For Love of a Donkey

For Love of a Donkey

Written and illustrated by

BETTY MORGAN BOWEN

DAVID McKAY COMPANY, INC.

NEW YORK

FOR LOVE OF A DONKEY

To

BERTHA L. GUNTERMAN

For Love of a Donkey

Chapter 1

EVERY TIME Karin looked at her donkey, she thought, How lovely!

Sometimes she sighed, or said, "Oh!" or whispered his name, "Bellissimo," a word which means "most beautiful." She could not look at his huge furry ears or his lustrous eyes or his brownish-gray curly sides without smiling.

She was never cross with him, not even now when he was standing with his legs as stiff as fence posts, refusing to go one step nearer the stream. She backed up to him and pushed him with such force that if he had moved, she would have sat down hard on the path.

"Silly old thing," she scolded. "You can't see your hoofs for mud. You're all muddy on one side, and you won't let me wash it off."

Bellissimo hated water. When thirst drove him to drink, he would touch the surface with the very tips of his lips and give a snort.

At the moment he was not thirsty. He pawed the ground and twitched his ears as if to say, "Not even for you will I go near that cold, bubbly, revolting stuff!" When Karin stopped for breath, he wheeled round to face the opposite way, where the meadow lay bright and inviting. Karin loosened his saddlebags and set him free.

Bellissimo sprang away. He raced twice around the meadow and dashed to the center of it to lie down and roll, braying loudly.

"This is my meadow and this is my time!" his brays declared. "This is Donkey Time!"

Karin laughed and moved the saddlebags away from the muddy path. They were not especially heavy now but clumsy, bulging with the twigs and branches she had been gathering. She swung the bags through the ferns and onto a slab of rock farther along the stream's edge. A branch worked loose and fell into a round pool. She stooped, picked it up, and paused, staring down. Karin caught her breath.

The pool was dark, shaded by trees, and there, reflected in the water, was a row of little girls. Karin knew they were only a reflection. Hadn't she herself sewn the figures onto the saddlebags, giving dozens, hundreds of hours to cutting them out and hemming and embroidering them, all because her donkey must have the handsomest pair of saddlebags in Germany?

But now the wavelets stirred up by the branch swayed the reflections and the pool turned into a festival. Ten little figures danced against a back cloth of fern whorls—and one of them looked exactly like her sister Gerti!

Karin smiled into the pool. She let herself down onto the moss and poked her finger into the water. How the figures danced! How their hair glinted, how their faces

shone, how their costumes glistened! Karin kicked off her
sandals and dug her toes into the moss. She closed her eyes
and wished—oh, it was impossible, it was like wishing for
Heaven to begin now. But when you've lost everything,

even your family, small wishes are no use; you wish tremendously, for great things to happen!

And so she wished that the figures would come to life,
that they would turn into her own family, that everything
would be just as before.

What a giant cluster of wishes to spring from a single
yearning!

She opened her eyes, only to narrow slits. The figures

swam hazily below her. She pretended her wishes had come true.

Then it happened: the first of the events which were to change Karin's life.

Another face joined the reflections in the pool, an old face with a white mustache and cheeks a mesh of tiny wrinkles. Karin's dream plummeted down into the black water. She shivered as if an icy fingertip had touched her neck. Her eyes looked up over the brink of the pool. The face was there, an old man was there, stepping out from the shadows on the opposite bank of the stream.

She burrowed her arm deep, deep in the cold water. Her glance widened to a blank enormous look.

"Good afternoon! I'm sorry! Coming out at you like this all at once—I've frightened you! Please don't be frightened!"

The old man spoke in German and Karin could understand every word. But he turned German into funny lilting music. Where had she heard a voice like his before? Karin raised herself on one elbow.

"Ah—excuse me, I am looking for a young lady named Karin Steiner," said the old man.

"I'm Karin Steiner." She was too afraid to stand up. What did this mean? She had made her wishes, and an old man had stepped out from between the trees. There he stood, saying her name. He might be a gnome or a goblin! Her thoughts flicked to stories she had read of gnomes and goblins—and elves. He might be an elf. He was small enough, but thin, dressed in a black suit. A tiny red ladybird was on his lapel. That was odd, but real enough. He even carried a gray hat and a black umbrella. Yet, surely, he was no ordinary old man. Swinging from his watch chain was a curious crystal object which sent out colored lights. The woods were full of spots of light, shining as if the stars had lost their way and come to earth in the daytime.

She expected him to disappear, she expected to find she was dreaming. It was all surely part of the dream about the little girls in the water. . . .

"Karin Steiner, aged eleven, living at Globkes' farm outside Julich, between Aachen and Cologne, in the Western Zone of Germany." The old man read from the card he drew from his waistcoat pocket.

"Yes." Karin stared across at the card. How could it say so much on a tiny card like that?

"And those handsome figures on your carriers there. Did you make them?"

"I—yes. Fräulein Krone helped. They're—" She heard the faint thud of hoofs. A jab of fear drove the color from her face. Bellissimo! She scrambled to her feet, knocking against the saddlebags so that more branches fell into the water. For months now she had been living in dread that someone would come to take Bellissimo away from her. She dreamed about it at night and woke to find herself screaming. She glanced over her shoulder every little while when she took Bellissimo to gather wood, and when she returned to Globkes' farm, she hid him where he could not be seen from the road.

She had gone cold to the soles of her feet, but there was a fiery dance of fears in her head, all for Bellissimo. She glanced through the trees. Bellissimo had come as far as the edge of the meadow. He was rubbing his side against the trunk of a tree.

The old man seemed not to have seen the donkey—or was he pretending? He picked his way over the steppingstones crossing the stream. He came closer to study the saddlebags.

"A French girl, I see, and a Finnish one, and that dark-haired one must be Greek, am I right? But the little one at the end is German, I'm sure. How did you know about the costumes?"

"Fräulein Krone told me. I live with Fräulein Krone, you see. She used to be a dressmaker." Karin stole a second glance through the trees.

"And the cloth? Where did you find all these colored scraps, so soon after the war?"

Now Karin blushed. "We found them in a sack in the Globkes' house—that's where we're staying. We think the Globkes must be dead, you see. No one has come back. I hope it's all right. They were such small scraps. The white cloth for the—the carrier—" The old man had called them carriers. He mustn't know they were saddlebags. "That white cloth was given to me. It's nylon from a parachute."

Karin's ears strained for sounds from Bellissimo. How could she lead the old man away, back across the stepping stones and along the far side of the stream so he would not see Bellissimo?

The old man touched the white cloth. He nodded approvingly; she had given the bags two thicknesses to make them strong. He said, "These carriers seem so large and heavy for a child to carry—"

Now what could she say? Now he would surely find out about Bellissimo!

Then, suddenly, it was too late. There was a snuffling noise. The old man gave a startled jump. Up flew his arms. Bellissimo pushed his way through the ferns, caring enough about Karin to come quite close to the water, much as he loathed it.

"A donkey!" the old man laughed. "I thought all the beasts of the forest must be after us!"

Watchful, intent, Karin said slowly, "This is Bellissimo. He's been in the meadow." She bent forward, poising almost off balance, ready to throw herself onto Bellissimo's back and gallop away.

"Bellissimo. A fine name for a gentleman donkey dressed in a collar of ferns," said the old man. He watched Bellissimo thrust his nose under Karin's arm. The donkey waggled his ears as if to try them out as wings, with the idea of carrying Karin soaring into the air.

Karin picked up the saddlebags, resting their connecting strap on her shoulder.

"I must go now. Fräulein Krone expects us back before the sun goes down," she said breathlessly. She stood like a sentinel between the old man and her donkey.

"I'll come with you," the old man said. "I've called at the farm already and left my case. Let me help you buckle on the bags."

He took off his hat and placed it, together with his umbrella, on the ground. He laid the strap connecting the saddlebags across Bellissimo's back. He reached for the girth straps and bent to buckle them.

Now that the old man wasn't looking at her, Karin dared to study him closer. She stared spellbound at his gray-gloved fingers working as gently as if he were tying a ribbon round a baby's neck, at his hair that was like a band of rabbit fur round his head. She thought again about his voice, how like funny tunes his sentences were. She had heard someone else speak like that. Who was it? She could not remember.

When the saddlebags were in place, the old man scratched the donkey's ears in the way Bellissimo liked best.

"People see a donkey," he said, "and they think, There's a donkey. Funny, stupid, stubborn old thing! They've no idea how clever a donkey is. When you know one well, you can tell from the way he holds his ears whether he's sad or happy. You can tell from the way he switches his tail whether he's content or angry or merry or distressed."

The old man knew about donkeys! He understood and liked them! Karin gulped in amazement. Her anxiety for Bellissimo vanished. She ran her fingers through his mane and began to confide in the old man as she never would have confided in Fräulein Krone.

"Yes," she said eagerly, "what you say is true! All donkeys are nice, but Bellissimo is really a most unusual donkey. He carries heavy loads without grumbling. He goes a long, long way without getting tired. He picks a path over the narrowest places without stumbling. If I leave him somewhere he always waits for me. But the most amazing thing

is—" She glanced at the old man. Shyness caught at her;
but he was smiling so warmly she was able to finish:

"Sometimes—almost always—when I look at Bellissimo,
I can tell exactly what he's thinking!"

"And what is he thinking?"

"Oh, he's thinking about eating usually. But sometimes—"

"Sometimes?"

"Sometimes he tells me things and I can understand quite
well. He even knows how to laugh!"

"I've heard of dogs laughing."

"Well, Bellissimo laughs. He looks at me and his eyes get
all twinkly and he lifts his head and laughs!"

"You must show me how he laughs," said the old man.

"Yes, I will," promised Karin. But the cheerfulness faded
from her face. She remembered that it had been a long time
since she and Bellissimo had laughed together. The laughing was no more than a memory from before the bombing
of Julich. Maybe her donkey had forgotten how to laugh.

Bellissimo trotted off to his beloved meadow. The old man
picked up his hat and umbrella, and he and Karin followed,
watching Bellissimo canter in a sweeping circle, making use
of his time until Karin should catch up to him.

At the edge of the meadow the old man stopped and
turned to Karin.

"You must excuse me. I was so pleased to find you that I
forgot to introduce myself. I'm afraid I have such a long
name that my friends just call me Professor—more than ever
now that I've retired and am not strictly a professor any
more."

Solemnly they shook hands. Karin noticed that the lady-bird was still on the old man's lapel. She wondered if it was make-believe. She thought that the crystal swinging from his watch chain might be a diamond.

"And now," said Professor, "I have something important to tell you. I've come to take you to Switzerland. I have given myself the task, the pleasure of escorting you to the Children's Village."

"The Children's Village," repeated Karin in a low voice. She couldn't understand at all. This man, this Professor who was smiling so happily, must surely be an elf! She had made a wish and now here was an elf, popped out from nowhere to take her back with him to Elfland!

He couldn't be an elf! she decided. Whoever heard of an elf dressed in a black suit and shiny black shoes and a gray hat and carrying a black umbrella?

Bellissimo came back. Karin held out her arms and he walked into them, thrusting his muzzle over her shoulder to sniff at Professor.

There was a shout, "Hey there!"

Karin tugged the donkey back. "What was he doing? I've never known him to—"

"He's under the impression that the mustache which I've trimmed so carefully over the past twenty years is a tasty new kind of grass, that's all!"

Professor was not angry. He was laughing, stroking Bellissimo as before, careful, though, not to bring his face too near. Her chin on her donkey's curly head, Karin gazed at Professor in awe.

"I found a big brush at Globkes'," she said, "and every morning I give him a good brushing. And sometimes I polish his hoofs. I wish I had a comb and I could comb his mane and his tail tuft. When we're on the way to—to Switzerland—I think I should bathe his hoofs in cool water every night. He won't like it but it will be soothing for him, don't you think so?

There was a sharp silence. Professor's next words struck Karin like a hard slap.

"He's *your* donkey?"

"Yes, of course. My father gave him to me. He brought him back from Italy. It was the last time, before he went away. He—"

Karin stopped speaking, caught by the look which seemed so out of place on Professor's face.

"But we can't take the donkey. It would be quite impossible to take him. No one told me you owned a donkey. I assumed he belonged to your—your Fräulein whoever-she-is! We're to fly to Switzerland, you and I! All the arrangements are made!"

A cloud moved in over the meadow and they walked under it toward Globkes' farm. Bellissimo walked between Karin and Professor, as close to Karin as he could without jostling her with the saddlebags. The pine trees at each side of the path to the farm were black giants. A wind followed them, sliding up from the ground, chilling their legs.

Karin began to hurry. She hurried faster and faster, wanting to dash free from the man who threatened to separate her from Bellissimo. She longed to climb on her donkey and

run away, but where, where? If she hid in the woods—
Winter would come and she and Bellissimo would die of
hunger and cold.

She was more afraid than she had been for many days.
Faster and faster she went, until she was running. Bellissimo
stayed at her side, jolting his bags. Now when she glanced
sideways, beyond Bellissimo, there was nothing but trees.
They had left the old man behind.

She looked back over her shoulder. Yes, there he was, she
saw with prickling alarm. But he was not running after her.
He had stopped. She could see him clearly against the strip
of sky beyond the meadow.

Something about him, the way he stood, hunched and
bowed, leaning on his umbrella, caught at Karin and made
her stop, too. Bellissimo turned back to her, nuzzling her
shoulder. She waited in the shadows, watching Professor
straighten his back and gaze upward. She thought she saw
his lips move as if he were whispering to someone.

Dazed with wondering, shivering a little, she went back
a few steps on her toes. She waited for Professor to rejoin
her, and walked with him all the way to Globkes' farm.

Chapter 2

Globkes' farm, where Karin had been living with Fräulein Krone since Julich had been bombed, was a brick building arranged on three sides of a square. It had been a fine farm; its flower beds were bordered by low brick walls; there were two barns, and fields spreading in all directions. The two chimneys of the farmhouse still rose proudly. But the barns were razed to the ground and the house had been burned. Now it lay mouldering, crusted with weeds and creepers, and open to the sky except for three rooms of one wing. It was to the first of these rooms that Karin led Professor. Bellissimo stationed himself outside, poking his head far enough through the window to see into every corner.

It was a poor room. There was a clumsy black iron stove in one corner, there was a broken table. There were boxes for chairs. The walls were cracked; the plaster had fallen in patches from the ceiling. And Fräulein Krone, stirring the pot on the stove, was as dismal as the room. She had met Professor when he arrived at the farm an hour before. Now she gave him the smallest nod and turned her back to him.

There were potatoes and cabbage for supper, and make-

believe coffee—and then the unbelievably fine box of chocolates which Professor brought out of the suitcase he had left
by the door. Karin tried to eat everything set before her.
But the cloud that had drifted over the meadow clung to
her and swam in her head, building up blacker inside her
each time she raised her knife and fork. All the while Fräulein Krone talked, her mouth turned down bitterly, her
small steely eyes glinting. She told Professor about the bombing of Julich, about how she had escaped and lived here and
there, wherever she could, about how she had come out along
the road and found Karin and the donkey at Globkes' farm.

"This room," she said, "think of it! Still with curtains in
the window, though of course there's no glass. We've been
lucky to have a roof over our heads, even a leaky roof. All
is gone, we've lost everything, you understand. If it weren't
so far out in the country we'd have a dozen people trying
to move in with us! And then finding the cabbages still in
the field, and the potatoes, sack upon sack of them in the
cellar under this very room! That's one reason why I'll be
glad to have the donkey. As soon as you and the child go I
shall set off myself to find my sister in Cologne. I'll need
the donkey to carry what's left of the potatoes. Nobody
knows how valuable potatoes have become since the bombing. Why, these days, people walk dozens of miles into the
country for a few pounds of potatoes!"

The black cloud extinguished everything, even Fräulein
Krone's voice. Karin's head drooped. She had no wish to
eat, or lift her hands from her lap, or even to take the next
breath. Bent forward over her plate, she grew aware dimly

that Professor was scraping back his chair and standing up. Through the billowing in her head she heard him say:

"Fräulein Krone, you are a selfish woman! When you told the welfare people about Karin and asked to have her taken away, why didn't you say that she owns a donkey, that this donkey was her last present from her father, that she values it more than anything else in the world! Now all the plans have been made, I have promised to be in Zurich in five days without fail, and it is impossible for us to take the donkey with us. I am distressed and angry. If I had known what I know now I would have planned otherwise. I would have moved Heaven and earth to take the donkey with us!"

For a moment longer Karin sat still, holding her breath, while the black cloud moved into her eyes, into her throat. She tried to swallow the cloying dankness.

Then with a whispered cry, "I—can't!" she threw herself from her chair and ran from the room. She rushed to Bellissimo, drew her arms around his neck and whispered in a hard dry voice:

"I can't! I can't leave you! You'll turn your face to the wall, you won't eat or drink any more, you'll die, Bellissimo, I know it! And I shall die, too, missing you!"

She didn't cry. She had not been able to cry since the shock of losing her family. But she rubbed her forehead sore against Bellissimo's fur.

"Karin—"

She looked up. Professor stood opposite, stroking Bellissimo's ear. Karin's heart gave a sharp lurch. The sun had come out in time to set. It shone on Professor's hands, on his bald pate, on his white mustache, on his dazzling smile!

"It's impossible, it's quite impossible! I don't know how we shall do it, but we shall find a way," he said. "We shall take your Bellissimo with us!"

Chapter 3

PACKING UP to leave was not difficult. The clothes she wore and Bellissimo with his saddlebags—these were Karin's only possessions. Most of the preparations had to do with Bellissimo.

First he had to be bathed. Swinging a bucketful of water from the well in the courtyard, Karin swooped down on her donkey. She climbed onto a platform of rubble, dumped the water over his back and jumped down to scrub him with the stiff brush she had found. All the while she murmured to him in bursts of confidence:

"Leave you behind, Bellissimo? Set off for Switzerland without you? No more going with you to gather wood, and feeling your funny old forelock tickling under my arm?"

Bellissimo's head drooped. His ears flopped forward. Karin leaned close and whispered into a furry ear:

"Not we! We'll never leave you, Professor and I! I promise you we'll never sell you or give you away or leave you behind, not anywhere, not any time!"

Then she laughed because, wet and bedraggled though he was, Bellissimo perked up, the spring came back into his legs, the mournfulness went out of his eyes. He gave a shake that sent Karin scuttling out of a bath-water shower.

Professor came out of the farmhouse and stretched himself in the sun, under a sky as clear as the pool where the little figures had danced. He watched Karin polish Bellissimo's hoofs and smooth layers of burlap sacking on his back. Again he helped Karin buckle on the saddlebags, and this time he fingered the straps, especially the one which crossed Bellissimo's back. It was of softest leather, and lined with fleece.

"The soldier gave me the straps. They used to be his parachute harness," Karin said quickly, so that Professor would not think she had taken them from the farmhouse. She thought it curious how he stroked them now. "Did he? You must tell me more about this soldier."

Professor brought his belongings from his suitcase and packed them into the saddlebags. Into one he put clean shirts and underwear, a stack of handkerchiefs and towels and soap; into the other, three big bars of chocolate, two loaves of bread, a jar of honey and boxes of butter and cheese. Bellissimo craned his neck to watch. He was still flicking his skin here and there to get rid of the wetness.

"Is he stubborn?" Professor asked, thinking about the journey ahead.

"Not a bit!" said Karin.

"And does he never kick or bite?"

"Once," whispered Karin behind her hand, "he nipped Fräulein Krone."

Professor winked at Bellissimo. "But how do you control him?" he asked. "There's no sign of a bridle or a halter."

"He had a lovely bridle and saddle once. It was a small saddle, made of leather and yellow felt," said Karin. "But we can lead him quite well without a bridle. I just walk in front and he follows. Once he followed me into the house and we had to move all the furniture to get him out again. Or we can lead him by the tail if you like."

Karin gave Bellissimo's tail a tweak. He walked forward. She tugged. He stopped.

"But he'd rather not be guided by his tail," she said. "It hurts his pride. He knows he's too clever for that, you see. Usually I just tell him what to do and he understands."

Bellissimo pawed the ground, eager to be off. He tossed his head. He seemed to be trying to curvet like a show horse.

"I hope he likes trains," said Professor. "Today's Monday. We must be at the Children's Village by three o'clock on Saturday afternoon. I've made a solemn promise to be in Zurich at six. That gives us five days. We should manage it with time to spare if we can board a train at Aachen."

Karin's fingers trembled as she washed her face and ears and neck at the well, smoothed her hair as tidily as she could with no comb or brush, and put on her wooden-soled sandals. Her heart pumped hard as she turned to the farmhouse door to bid Fräulein Krone good-by.

"Thank you for taking care of me." She kissed Fräulein Krone's cheek and curtsied. She could not bring herself to look into Fräulein Krone's eyes.

"A fine way you have of showing your thanks," said Fräulein Krone.

Professor stepped forward.

"Please accept my suitcase with all good wishes for a pleasant journey to Cologne and an early reunion with your sister."

"I'm to have a pleasant journey, I suppose, with a heavy case in one hand and a great sack of potatoes on my back," said Fräulein Krone. "And you're asking for trouble, thinking of going hundreds of miles down the length of Germany with a child and a donkey. You'll tire before you've gone a mile. You'll collapse in the road and then what will the child do? What good will the donkey be to her then?"

Professor's face grew red, his eyes round. The tips of his mustache pointed out like spears. He waited for the woman to finish.

"And there's another thing I didn't tell you. She's a problem at night. She cries out in her sleep and gets up from her bed and goes to see the donkey. And three times I've caught her sleepwalking! And one more thing! How will you get the donkey over the border? Have you exit and entry permits for it? Do you think the border police will let a donkey out of one country into another with no permits? You had best think again, old man, before you set off!"

Karin stood aghast, not daring to look up. Fräulein Krone had shouted at Professor as if he were an ordinary old man! An ordinary old man, when it might be he had only to lift his watch chain for the crystal to smite her to stone on the doorstep!

But all he did was to give a stiff bow.

"Thank you for your advice," he said. "It's exactly what one would expect from a foolish and very selfish old woman!

And now I bid you farewell!" He swung his watch chain and a spot of magenta light settled on Fräulein Krone's long nose. Karin held her breath.

"I bid you farewell, then!" Fräulein Krone turned, stamped into the house, and banged the door.

Professor put on his hat and gloves and they walked away, through the shadows of the farmhouse chimneys and down the grassy overgrown path. It was so soft and springy that there were merely little scuffling sounds from eight feet walking, and the gentle rustling of the saddlebags.

At first only Bellissimo was happy. He wuffled his nose and tossed his head and pranced. Excitement stirred up the first "eee-a" he had brayed that day. He liked the sound. He lifted his head and brayed again, mightily this time, "Eee-a! Eeee-ah! EEEE-AHH!"

The path turned into a dirt lane, then into a pebbly road. Now Bellissimo's hoofs made a clippity-cloppity sound. The grasses bowed, the breezes stroked past, primroses nodded in hundreds and thousands, and the sky promised to keep clear until night. The sun turned Professor's crystal into a fairy charm. Colored blobs of light hopped and skipped along as if hurrying to keep pace; and it was this, Karin decided, that made the birds sing. Overhead and on the roadsides, before them and behind them—it seemed that all the birds in Germany must be near, fluttering and singing merrily.

Karin began to hear music in her head, a bumpy donkey tune which lightened her feet and swung her arms forward and back. Professor made up a poem:

"Early one morning in May we set out,
And nobody knew we were about,
But the birds, and how they sang to say,
God bless you all along your way!"

"How funny!" exclaimed Karin. "Your poem fits the tune that's been going round and round in my head!"

"Hum it then!" urged Professor.

Hesitantly Karin hummed the tune, twice through. Professor set the poem to it and he and Karin sang it over and over, and laughed because it was a merry tune, because the words fitted it perfectly, because with every step the sky looked bluer and wider and more beautiful.

Yet at the brow of the next hill Karin stopped singing and dropped behind, scraping her sandals against the pebbles. How was it that not once until now had she realized they were on their way to Julich? Even here, half a mile away, she could see the crumpled ruins of her town. Somewhere in that mass of gray rubble was her home, and the school, and the church, and the home of Marianne, her best friend, and the corner by the shop where she had kissed her father good-by for the last time, when he had brought her Bellissimo for a present.

"Take care of him, Karin. You're his mistress now. Never let him go hungry or thirsty."

Those had been her father's words.

She had not been back to Julich since the week of the bombing. The first day she had run back from the fields where she had been with Bellissimo. She had fought her way through the smoke and dust haze to find no one, nothing, where her home and her mother and sister had been. She had gone back five times before she had finally run away with Bellissimo.

Professor, Karin and the donkey came down into Julich. The line of houses began, but they weren't houses. They were nothing but broken pieces of wall. Sometimes there was a window frame and through it one could see the sky. How very still it was, this little town that was no longer a town, this road that was no longer a road, but only a path through hills of rubble! To walk along it was to go through people's homes, through the lives of people Karin had known. Here lived Trude, here Horst, here the three Klein boys who looked alike—and here Marianne. What had happened to Marianne?

Karin wanted to tell Professor about Marianne, about how Marianne had gone everywhere with her, a tiny, bright, comical girl who made the whole town laugh. Quickly and breathlessly she said:

"I—had a friend, Marianne Meister. She lived on this corner. I think it was here. Every day I wonder about her. I know her parents were lost. She herself wasn't in Julich that day. I keep hoping she's all right."

They reached the place where her own house had stood. Strangely, the cherry tree was still there, a mass of pink bloom. How could a cherry tree go on living when everything else was gone?

Karin turned in and walked across what had been the front garden. She climbed over lumps of stone and plaster and cement and sketched out with her eyes the plan of the house. She pulled herself over the hump of front wall and crossed the living room. She walked like a ghost through the wall into the kitchen and back again.

"All is gone—all—all," she whispered. Already soil was silting in and the strong stalks of bay-willow-herb sprang up where the carpets had been.

"Was it there you lived?" Professor asked understandingly.

Karin nodded. "All is gone."

"Come."

She went back to Professor and Bellissimo.

They continued along the narrow path through Julich. They saw not so much as a dog or cat; they heard nothing but their own footfalls.

At the far end of the town Karin stopped once more and stared back along the lines of fallen houses. "I'm going— father—mother—Gerti. I am going far away. Till we meet again." Her shoulders hunched, her fists clenched her ragged pullover. Professor went on a distance without her.

"Nothing left, nothing," she muttered huskily. She pushed back her hair and hurried her steps to catch up to Professor. Before she could reach him she saw him stumble and barely manage to catch himself. Fear set her feet running. Professor was tiring. The trip was already too hard for him. Fräulein Krone had been right. He would collapse in the road! And there was no one to be seen in Julich. Where could she take him, what could she do?

She ran to him and grasped him by the arm. She realized in astonishment and for the first time that he was a bent, wizened old man, not much taller than she herself.

"You're ill, Professor?" she whispered. "You want me to get help?"

He shook his head. He tried to smile. His chin was trembling and there were tears among the wrinkles under his eyes.

"You're—crying!" she breathed. "Why are *you* crying?"

He brought out his handkerchief. He straightened himself and gave a huge shrug. He blew his nose and tried again to smile. All at once she knew he was crying because of the war, because it had killed and hurt people. She knew how he felt, she could understand if anybody could!

She put her arm around him to comfort him, and like that they walked slowly away from Julich, out into the open country and on toward Aachen.

Chapter 4

THEY WALKED so quietly along the Aachen road that they surprised a rabbit into a jump, a hare into a vault, a flock of crows into flapping, cawing flight. On a curve of road in the stillest of countrysides, they stopped for a picnic. Bellissimo began to graze and for a little while Karin and Professor sat by the roadside, their feet in the grassy ditch. They listened to the buzzing of insects and gazed across neglected fields to the misty hills beyond. How wide and endless the world looked! What a long way it must be to the very southern tip of Germany!

Karin thought about the events of today and yesterday. So much had happened that was odd: Her wish, Professor's appearing among the trees, his knowing a great deal about her without her saying a word— Who was he? Why had he come to find her? How had he known so surely where she would be, even with Fräulein Krone's appeal to the welfare people? What kind of place was this Children's Village he talked about?

It was all so odd and frightening. To dash her fears away, Karin jumped up from the ditch and busied herself unbuckling Bellissimo's straps, slipping the bags and sacks from his back. He shook himself and sniffed the air approvingly. He did not trot straightway into the field, but thrust his head at Karin to be patted.

Professor was watching. "Do you know," said Karin, "sometimes Bellissimo wakes out of a sound sleep under a tree and comes to me and then, when I've patted him, he walks back under the tree and goes to sleep again."

She gave him a scratch behind both ears, and as she did it, she asked Professor, "Do you think he's perhaps a bit thin for a donkey?"

"He's as healthy as any donkey I've met," said Professor. "How have you managed to feed him and keep him warm all through the winter?"

Karin sighed.

"I couldn't do it very well. I put him in the room next to the stove. There wasn't enough dried grass. I spent an hour every day pulling grass, you see. Then I dried it and put it away for the winter." She took hold of her donkey's cheeks and looked him in the eye.

"You're a good fellow," she said. "You never complain, and I know you like beets best—and bran mash and chaff and oats. Go ask Professor if they have those things for donkeys in Switzerland."

Bellissimo stepped nearer the road to thrust his muzzle down the back of Professor's neck. The old man clapped both hands over his mustache.

"He's nuzzling you just as he does me!" exclaimed Karin. "He's never nuzzled anyone else like that except my friend Marianne. It means he likes you! I'm glad. I'm sure he knows you saved him from Fräulein Krone. Think of an animal being that clever!"

Karin clapped Bellissimo on the thigh.

"Go on now, you funny donkey. There's green grass and a shady tree to stand under and—" She swept her arm out over the field. "Oh, but I wonder—" She grew silent, asking herself if this place had been cleared of mines. She darted a glance at Professor's smiling face, at the crystal she was almost sure was magic.

She decided the field was safe. She called to Bellissimo who was already deep in the field. "I think there's a stream down there—there beyond that old barn."

She stared at the barn, blinked and opened her mouth in surprise. *The* barn! How was it she hadn't noticed until now? This was the field, that was the very barn where she had found the soldier!

She carried the saddlebags to Professor and sat down near him, but without looking at him, without daring to look. Who was he? Why had he decided to stop here, so near that barn, when there were miles and miles of fields to choose from, and dozens and dozens of barns? Did he know everything, absolutely everything about her?

Professor drew out his penknife and cut four chunks of bread from one of the loaves. He cut slices of cheese and spread butter thickly over the bread. Before the war Karin had eaten lots of good things, but she could remember nothing as delicious as Professor's fine white bread and real butter and soft yellow cheese.

Yet good as it tasted, the bread and cheese stayed un-

chewed in her mouth. She was baffled, she couldn't understand Professor or the journey or anything that had happened since he had found her. She sat still, looking straight
ahead across the road. Sometimes she took a deep breath.

She thought about how furious Professor had been with
Fräulein Krone. Why, if he were an elf or a pixie of some
sort, had he not put a magic spell on her to turn her to a
frog or a toad or maybe nothing more than a small black
beetle?

She pictured him standing alone on the path to Globkes'
farm. He had looked up and moved his lips as if speaking
to someone. To whom, to the King of Elfland? To the Fairy
Queen? Or perhaps to God?

She remembered how a few days before the bombing, she
and her mother had been talking about Heaven. Her mother
had said, "Daddy's waiting for us in Heaven. And some day
we'll go there ourselves, and see him, and be together for
always."

Mother and Gerti had gone to Heaven. They were with
Daddy.

Suddenly Karin's stomach froze. She coughed and coughed
and her face went red and tears sprang to her eyes. Professor
bent over her and patted her back.

Soon it was better. Karin cleared her throat and rubbed
her forehead. Still Professor bent over her, serious and yet
smiling.

"What happened? Did some bread go down the wrong
way?"

Karin shook her head. She glanced at Professor, away and

then back again. She had not noticed before how extraordinary his eyes were, how very light, like burnished silver. And how brilliant they were, bright as the darts of light from his crystal.

He was surely a guardian angel. When they reached Heaven he would leave her and go in search of another lonely child. But that would be all right because she would be with Mother and Daddy and Gerti. He wouldn't leave her at the gates, or on the steps. He'd stay with her all the way.

Oh, but she was afraid. The air had gone chill, her feet and hands were cold and clammy. She wanted to jump on Bellissimo and ride away—back—anywhere!

"What is it, Karin? You've gone so pale. Are you all right?" How closely he studied her! His eyes gleamed into hers.

She gulped again and hung her head.

"I thought—it seemed—" she faltered. Desperately she changed the subject. She had not meant to mention the barn, but now it sprang into her mind like a promise of safety.

"It's funny we've stopped here," she said.

"Why?"

"Because over there is the barn where I found the soldier."

Professor shaded his eyes. He studied the deserted farm, the ruined farmhouse, the barn with half its roof gone. Rather than sit down again to go on with his picnic, he said, "I think I'll walk over there and have a look around."

He strolled away, leaving his hat and his umbrella be-

hind. He didn't expect Karin to follow him and he was surprised when he heard her voice behind him in the barn
doorway. But she had to tell him.

"He was in the second stall, the one with the door," she
said timidly. "He wouldn't let me come in. He said once a
little girl bit him on the arm. He laughed a lot. He made me
laugh. Oh, he was nice. His name was Philip. I brought him
water and blackberries and potatoes. I found the potatoes in
the farmhouse. He threw me his box of matches and I made
a fire outside and cooked the potatoes. We both ate a lot.
He said some day he'd come back to Germany and find me.
I liked him very much, but I never saw him, at least not
clearly. I never saw his face. That's very strange, isn't
it?"

They opened the door to the stall where the soldier had
stayed. Bellissimo trotted into the barn and straight to the
trough along its wall to lick up the last of the oats lying
there.

"Well, would you believe it? That funny donkey remem-
bers being here before!" said Karin. She turned back to the
stall in time to see Professor pluck a shining object from the
straw and thrust it swiftly into his pocket. She was almost
sure it was a watch. She waited for Professor to say something about it.

He kept silent. When they had gone out into the sun
again he asked, "How did he go away, do you know?"

"He asked me to find some soldiers and bring them to
him—not German soldiers but Americans or English or
Belgians. That's when he gave me the parachute and the

straps. He told me to hide them until after he'd gone away. I hid them in the first stall, deep under the hay. I came back for them afterwards."

They walked back to their picnic place at the roadside. Bellissimo passed them with a shake of ears and a switch of tail, on the way to the stream to drink.

"Tell me what you did," said Professor. "Did you find the soldiers?"

"I rode on Bellissimo, over the fields. I was afraid because of the mines. There were more mines then, you see. But I was more afraid on the roads. I was afraid somebody would take Bellissimo away. I went many miles, and then I saw some trucks and a jeep. I followed them, and when they stopped I hid Bellissimo and walked up to the soldiers in the jeep, and oh, I was afraid! I told them there was a soldier hiding in a barn. I said I would show them where he was but first they must promise not to take my donkey away. I rode Bellissimo back along the road and they followed in the jeep. It was night when we reached the barn. They went inside and I ran away." Karin shivered, remembering the darkness of the wood where she had hidden with Bellissimo, the black trees that soon grew too thickly for a donkey to squeeze between, the canopy of branches that shut every bit of starlight away.

Professor took up his sandwich. He said:

"You are a brave young lady. I pronounce you worthy to become a member of the Children's Village. And now you may pin on your badge." He brought from his waistcoat pocket a card on which was stuck a make-believe ladybird like the one he wore on his lapel. As Karin pinned it to her pullover, he continued:

"I want to tell you about the Children's Village. I've just spent some weeks there. I wanted to find the right place for you to spend your future, and I think this is the most wonderful little village in the whole world. It's full of children from many nations, living happily together. There's no hunger and no loneliness. I'm glad to have a chance to take you there. I'm glad I found you. How marvelous it was to come upon you there by the stream! It was like diving down, straight down and picking up a pearl from the sea floor, I came to you as directly as that—and from such a long way off."

A wide, wide smile lit Professor's face and squeezed his eyes out of sight. He was so pleased, it was as if she were somebody really important, as if he had found a lost princess!

"We shall have a long, long journey," he said, "and somehow we must get Bellissimo across the border. That's my chief worry. If only we can manage that. We must manage it! We'll put all our determination into it! And then when we've crossed into Switzerland everything will be fine. We shall climb high, high up over the rim of the hills—and we shall be there!"

Karin pictured a fairy mountain shimmering with lights. She sighed, and wriggled her toes in her sandals. How amazing it all was! Somehow Professor had heard about her and had come a great distance, all for her. And he had saved Bellissimo for her. She must use all her courage not to be afraid but to keep on until they reached their destination.

And she must pray every night that Bellissimo would be allowed to cross the border. It wouldn't matter if the Children's Village was in Heaven or in Elfland or in Switzerland or some other strange place. What would matter was that she would keep Bellissimo with her, and she would never be hungry or lost or lonely again!

She picked up her sandwich and leaned back on one elbow. Relief and hope flowered into a huge smile.

Chapter 5

HALF THE loaf of bread still lay across Professor's knees when a row of children appeared, turning into the Aachen road from a track that ran past the derelict barn. First came a thin girl, older then Karin, bent under a potato sack, next came a boy with a bulging knapsack, and behind him three younger children carrying bags. Karin saw as they came nearer that they were attached to one another by a rope knotted from waist to waist.

They walked single file until the little girl in the middle of the line caught sight of the picnic and bounded forward, tangling the rope. The boy who was second in the row scolded her and shouted to the others in a sergeant-major voice. The eldest girl kept her eyes on the road and plodded on, tugging at the rope; but when the others stopped short near Karin and Professor, the rope went taut and the big girl was brought to a standstill.

"Look, Hildegard, look! Wait a minute!" The younger ones pulled their big sister back. They formed a semi-circle around Karin and Professor.

Sacks and bags were dumped in the road. The littlest ones —Karin could see now that they were twins, a boy and a girl—plunked themselves into the ditch, close to Professor's

feet and stared up at the crusty heel of the loaf poking out
over his knees. Karin reached out to them. They grasped her
hands and smiled, but their eyes went back to the bread.

"You've been walking a long way?" Professor asked the
big girl. He cut two slices from the loaf and Karin buttered
them, patted a piece of cheese onto each and handed them

to the twins. Professor went on cutting slices while the girl
talked.

"We've walked five miles from Aachen and now we must
walk back again. But we've bought two sacks of potatoes,
and we only spent the tablecloth and four cigarettes; we
didn't have to spend the ring. Mother will be very pleased!"

The girl stopped talking to eat her bread and cheese. She
and the others ate quickly. The only sound from them was

the steady chomping of jaws. Their eye flickered in the dazzling colors from the crystal. The bread disappeared— half a loaf barely made one slice apiece—and there was only a blob of butter melting on its paper. The children licked the corners of their mouths and studied the crystal.

Professor fingered it. "You're wondering," he said, "what makes it send out so many colors, is that right?"

Karin listened intently. Now perhaps the mystery would come clear: Who Professor was, why he had come to find her.

The line of faces moved closer to watch Professor lift his watch chain and twist it until blue and purple and red and yellow lights turned the ditch into a fairyland.

"This is a prism. It's been cut and polished with as much care as would go into the cutting of a diamond for a king's crown. I value it most of all my possessions."

Karin sighed. She knew now that the glittering pendant was called a prism. But the question remained: Was it magic or not?

The oldest girl moved closer to Karin.

"I never ate bread like that, never in my whole life," she murmured. "Where did he get it?"

"I don't know," whispered Karin.

All eyes went back to Professor as he reached into one of the saddlebags and brought out the second loaf of bread.

"We'll have a party," he said, "and let tomorrow take care of itself."

How the children enjoyed the bread spread with honey! They chewed and chuckled and talked all at once. They nudged one another, their eyes glinted. One said, "Wait till we get home and tell Mutti!"

For dessert there were the three bars of chocolate. The twins lay on their backs in the grass, their heads on the bags of dandelion leaves they had gathered to make soup. They lay still, sucking the chocolate. They did not chew. They wanted to keep the taste in their mouths as long as they could. When the last bit had slipped down their throats they held up dirty fingers to lick away the taste still left there.

The rope around the twins' waists was untied and Karin played with them in the grass. She crawled on all fours, barking like a dog and meowing like a cat. She pushed against them with her face and they laughed deep throaty laughs that made the others laugh, too. They rolled on the grass and began to fall asleep, side by side. Karin stroked their cheeks with one finger and thought about her sister Gerti.

"Look how their eyes droop shut and they try to open them and they droop shut again," she whispered to Professor. "And look, they're smiling at me, half asleep! Oh, Professor, I've just had an idea!"

Karin squeezed her hands together in earnestness.

"We can put the twins in Bellissimo's saddlebags! They won't hurt anything, and they can sleep as much as they like, jogging along! And the potatoes—I'm sure Bellissimo could carry them, both sacks of them! He loves to be useful!"

Where was Bellissimo? Karin jumped up and dashed away across the field. She found him in the ruined barn, looking for more oats. When Karin called him from the doorway, he opened his mouth in a noisy greeting. He

clomped across the field after her, sensing that he was to
have an important job to do, too full of business to race in
circles as he usually did to tease her. He trotted straight to
his saddlebags.

And soon he set off toward Aachen, with two sacks of
potatoes roped to his back and a twin in each saddlebag
with the Professor's things. His ears were cocked high and
one eye glinted sideways at Karin. He felt important. The
tick-tack, tick-tack of his hoofs said:

"Down through the valley and up o'er the rise,
I'm a young donkey who's clever and wise!"

Karin grinned at Bellissimo, hoping he would lift his
head and laugh as he used to do. She even tickled him and
giggled at him, but it was no use. He had surely forgotten
how to laugh.

They made a neat procession with Bellissimo in the center
and marchers at each side. They walked steadily along, talking a little. Karin asked the oldest girl if she knew anyone
named Marianne Meister. "A tiny girl, eleven years old,
very blonde and merry."

The big girl shook her head. "There's nobody very merry
where we live."

They reached Aachen in the late afternoon. At first, coming toward it down a steep hill, looking down on its ca-
thedral, Karin thought, The same beautiful town I remember! But as the procession drew near, the tiers of houses and
public buildings turned to shells, the rooms behind the shells
gutted and tossed heaps of rubble. Everywhere there was an
unpleasant smell of old fires and damp and decay. And

now, for the first time in months, Karin saw crowds of people. They wandered about or stood in little groups at the corners. They were pale and shabby and darkly dressed, like ghost people. There were ragged children everywhere, turning to stare and shout as Bellissimo went by. Karin studied them one by one, looking for Marianne.

"We are nearly there," said the big girl. "We live round the next corner, there in the bunker. One day," she added hastily, "we'll live in a house again."

Karin knew about the bunkers. They were air-raid shelters with walls six feet thick and no windows. She had never imagined that people could live in them day after day.

"Are there many people living in the bunkers?" she asked.

"Hundreds. Thousands, I think. In winter it's warm inside. And every day they give us bread and soup. That's worth something!"

The bunker children rushed out to see Bellissimo. They jumped up and down with glee.

"Look, a donkey, right in our yard!"

"It's a donkey, a real live donkey!"

They came closer, stretching out their hands to touch him and stroke him.

The big girl lifted the twins from the saddlebags and set them on their feet. They teetered sleepily, and rubbed their eyes with their fists. The sacks of potatoes were untied from Bellissimo's back and the big girl shook hands with Karin and Professor and kissed the donkey's furry cheek.

"We'll give you some potatoes," she offered.

"Oh, no, no! Nothing, thank you!" Professor began to

lead Karin and Bellissimo away. The children's mother came out of the bunker.

"You've dropped down from Heaven, you're God's angels, I really do believe it!" she exclaimed. "You must have some potatoes for your kindness!"

"No, no, thank you." Professor smiled.

The big girl held out the ring it had not been necessary to spend.

"My ring then," said the mother. "You must take it!"

"No, really, nothing, thank you. It's Bellissimo we must thank."

The mother wrung her hands. "But it's impossible that you should simply go away like this. Is there nothing at all we can do for you?"

"Nothing, thank you. God be with you." There was more handshaking. Karin and Professor had to stop again because the twins, wide awake now, held tight to Bellissimo's hind legs.

"My donkey! My donkey!" they cried in unison.

The other bunker children joined in with shouts of, "His name's Bellissimo! Isn't he wonderful? He carried Ewald and Trude all the way in his bags, and both sacks of potatoes as well!"

The mother and the big girl pried the twins loose from Bellissimo's legs, but they pulled free and hurled themselves at Karin. They refused to let go of her. They bunched her skirt into their fists. Their fingers had to be unclenched one by one.

"Stop here with us!" they begged. Karin could only shake

her head and smile as she moved away. There were howls of disappointment mixed with shouts and laughter. Even Bellissimo began to shout, "Eea! Eeeah!" It was difficult to get out of the bunker yard.

"God will bless your journey, you will see!" the mother cried after them. She went on shouting to the people in the yard, "If there were more folk like that old man and that child, there wouldn't be any wars!"

They walked deeper into the town, along narrow ways where jagged chunks of cement threatened to graze their shoulders as they passed. Professor stopped at a gray building and looked to the right and left before he led Karin and Bellissimo part way down the alley at one side.

"I must go in here to get some papers signed so you can cross into Switzerland," he explained. "And I shall try to get the permits for Bellissimo. Your papers should be ready. They've been going from desk to desk for days now. There's a big file labeled Karin Steiner. But I'm anxious about Bellissimo. If it means a delay— Well, we'll do our best. Wait here, Karin. Don't wander out into the road."

Karin and Bellissimo waited close to the building, near the door through which Professor had disappeared. Karin hoped no one would notice them. A man or a big boy, hungry and used to stealing since the war, could easily drag Bellissimo away. She listened to the footsteps on the road in front of the building; she heard voices rise and fall.

What a terrible town Aachen had become! It was as if a spoiled giant child had built a town of toy bricks, then kicked it over and gone away. And yet now, when no one seemed of any importance any more, the people in the office upstairs had a folder marked Karin Steiner. How had that happened?

Puzzling, leaning with her forehead against Bellissimo's neck, she remembered that one day at a farmhouse near Globkes' Fräulein Krone had exchanged a handkerchief for two sheets of paper, a stub of pencil and an envelope. Weeks later a man had come to Globkes' farm. He had brought a camera and taken two pictures of Karin. He had asked questions about her family.

In the folder upstairs, thought Karin, there must be the letter from Fräulein Krone, and the pictures the man took, and the sheet he filled with writing while he was asking questions. But how was it that Professor knew about the folder?

Weary of questioning, she shut her eyes. At first she thought she was dreaming when a voice called, "Hello there, little girl."

Alarmed, she pulled away from Bellissimo and peered into the rubble lining the alley. Farther back was a shadowy opening, and there sat an old woman, huddled on a box.

"Hello, dear! Come into the light! Let me see you, please!" The voice wavered. Karin took a few steps along the alley. Bellissimo followed like a watchdog.

She could see the old woman more clearly now. She could see the wrinkled face round itself to a toothless smile.

"Ahhh," came the trembling voice. "I could be looking at my own granddaughter!" The old woman did not stop gazing at Karin, though her head began to twitch slightly back and forth.

"What is your name?" she asked.

"Karin."

"It's not to be believed. You're so like my granddaughter. When I caught sight of you, I thought for an instant, Irmgard! It's my Irmgard!"

"You live here?" Behind the old woman was a tumble-down room. There was nothing in it but an iron bed and a table holding rusty pots and broken crockery.

The old woman shrugged.

"Yes, yes, all is gone," she said. "But at least I've found a little corner I can have for my own. It's better than living in the bunkers. Does the donkey belong to you?"

"Yes." Karin told the old woman that she and her donkey were on their way to Switzerland.

"Ah—. So—. You have a very great distance to go. But I have just the thing for your journey." The old women went into her room, searched among the things on the table and brought out to Karin a silver bell. It was cracked, but its note was as clear and true as Professor's May song. "For your donkey," said the old woman, "so you can always tell where he is and need never lose him on the way."

"How lovely! How kind you are! And I don't even know your name," said Karin.

"I'm Frau Lang. If you hear of someone named Lang on your travels—oh, but it's rather a common name. I shall have to wait here. I've told the housing people where I am. Perhaps one day I'll look up and my daughter and my grand-daughter will be here! But we must think how to attach the bell. I'm sorry I don't have a piece of string—"

Karin reached into the pocket of her skirt and brought out the small D-shaped metal object the soldier had given her many months before. It had been the handle for the rip-cord of his parachute. Karin had treasured it, and now it slipped through Bellissimo's girth strap and the bent loop on the crown of the bell as if it had been made for this purpose. With a stone she bent the loop tighter round the handle. The bell swung free and tinkled softly.

Karin wished she had something to give Frau Lang. It would not be right to give her something of Professor's without asking him first and she had nothing of her own to give. Then suddenly she found herself shaking hands good-by and hurrying away, forgetting to care about Frau Lang and her family, for Professor had come out of the building, and all that mattered was that Bellissimo should be allowed to cross the border.

"Is it all right about Bellissimo?" Her question tunneled its way down the alley. "Can we—?" She was nearer the door now, and let the sentence drop, her attention caught by Professor's pursed mouth, by his sagging shoulders.

"I must show you your passport, Karin," he said. "You're a very important person now, owner of a passport with a picture inside." He held the passport open at the photograph. There was a piece of Bellissimo's head in one corner of it.

"But Bellissimo," insisted Karin.

Professor turned toward the light at the top of the alley.

"He said there isn't a chance. He advises us to look for a good home for him, some farm or other outside Aachen. He said there isn't a chance in—"

"Oh, no!" whispered Karin.

"In a thousand!"

"And if we were to wait for the permits?"

"Three weeks, a month, longer, and even then the chances are we would be refused."

Professor took Karin by the arm, and she did not even think to wave to Frau Lang as she let herself be led out of the alley into the road. Bellissimo followed, his head low, his new bell ringing, his ears flopping like tags. At the first corner Professor stopped.

"I don't believe him. I don't believe that anybody, not even a border policeman, would be mean enough to take a child's pet away from her! I may be a foolish old man, but I think people's hearts are warmer than that, war or no war! I told the man so and he laughed at me!"

Karin didn't dare look into Professor's face. She looked only as far as his hands, which reached out to finger the parachute handle attaching Bellissimo's new bell.

"So what we must do, Karin," he said very softly, "is go forward, we three, and see what happens!"

He lifted his chin and set off again, taking bigger steps than before. But underneath he was so humble! Karin knew he was afraid they would be disappointed. She admired him and yet she pitied him. She found herself wanting to take care of him, as if he were the child and she the grownup. She—take care of wise, clever Professor who was eight or nine times her age—or perhaps hundreds of years old!

They walked on toward a building which rose like the blackened skeleton of a monstrous whale. The bones of the whale's ribs rose in sweeping arcs, some of them bent, some trailing, twisted and broken. Aachen Station had lost its roof and some of its walls. It was bleak and dirty, and overcrowded with tired people. There was no clock, and only a makeshift barrier. A train had just drawn in and masses of people were surging toward it, some running round the edges of the crowd and pushing their way in farther on. Soon the train was crammed, yet more people were trying to push their way in, and still more were running alongside, dragging their bundles and cases.

Karin, Professor and Bellissimo picked their way around piles of rubbish to join a long line of people waiting before the ticket window. Close to Karin, Bellissimo hung his ears down gloomily. Karin turned her back to the ticket window and watched the train pull out of the station. There were far too many people on board. There was shouting and pushing. Heads and arms thrust out of windows. Clusters of men balanced themselves on the buffers between the carriages.

Karin felt a twist of anxiety for Bellissimo. How could they get him safely to Switzerland if all the trains were like this one?

A switch engine thundered through the station. Its smoke forced its way down Karin's throat, its noise drove her thoughts away. She saw a red light flick to green and back to red. She watched two carriages come together on the opposite track. There was a jarring, rasping bump, a jingling of chains, and still the carriages weren't coupled. Men began to shout at one another. Everything was going wrong. The station was full of trouble.

An official hurried toward them. His face shiny with sweat, his nose quivering excitedly, he came to demand what they thought they were doing, bringing a donkey onto the station platform.

Professor explained that they had come to catch a train, that they wished to travel as quickly as possible to the Swiss border.

"You expect to take a donkey by train—in Germany—so soon after the end of the war?" demanded the official. "There are almost no trains running! There is hardly a goods train to be found anywhere! They are destroyed. They are abandoned here and there, bombed, thrown from the tracks!" The official flung his arms out. He spread his hands chest high and spoke loudly. The people near by circled round, forgetting about the line they had been forming. Bellissimo stamped his hoof, ringing his bell.

"And let's pretend we find a goods train somewhere," went on the official. "Right. It comes into Aachen. We put your donkey aboard. We attach his exit and entry permits to his saddlebags perhaps. What happens to the animal? We put him out somewhere, anywhere, and he crops grass until you appear, hey presto! It's all quite impossible! You must find some other way!" The official jabbed at the air with his thumb. He seemed to be trying to address the whole station, all the crowd waiting and wondering if another train would come soon.

The official tilted his head closer to Professor and dropped his voice. "At least you have passports and permits—to Switzerland, too! That alone is a dream come true, worth a fortune these days!"

Professor shrugged. "We haven't yet managed any permits for the donkey."

"No permits?" The man's voice rose again. "And you

expect to get that animal out of the country? Excuse me, but you must be crazy!"

Professor, Karin and Bellissimo trailed down the platform and out into the town once more.

"So—. Not to worry. We must find another way," said Professor.

But twin worries whirled in Karin's head. There was the worry about the permits, that they would make the journey the length of Germany only to find that it was impossible for Bellissimo to cross into Switzerland, and there was the fear that Professor would tire and grow ill on the way.

They walked across a ruined square, and a wind crept after them, rustling the rubbish at their heels; and night crept in after them. Professor held himself as erect as before, his shoulders back, his chin up, his glance darting about, missing nothing. Oh, but he was tired. Karin could tell from the dragging of his heels. He was an old, old man. He needed to rest. Where would they go? What would they eat now that the bread and butter and cheese and chocolate were gone? Where would they sleep tonight?

Karin moved closer to Bellissimo. She reached out to him and he gave her fingers a lick.

She looked across at Professor. He turned to her with his warm smile. She took a deep breath and stepped out more firmly. He had called her a brave young lady and had given her a ladybird badge. She must be sure to be worthy of it, no matter how awful the journey turned out to be!

Chapter 6

"To THE LEFT, Bellissimo. Watch that rough corner there. Now through the opening— Good boy, good Bellissimo." Karin whispered directions to a donkey too tired to prick his ears.

Did Professor have a plan or were they simply wandering on and on? Now he was asking his way to the Kurhaus, a beautiful hotel.

Rubbing her heel in the dust, not bothering to look up, she heard a voice say: "But it's no longer a hotel, you understand. Bombed, all knocked about, you understand."

They went on in growing darkness. Karin's feet hurt where the straps of her sandals rubbed. She tried not to limp, not to distress Professor.

"Please," she called over to him, "get on Bellissimo. Ride a bit. You're tired, I can tell."

"No, no, I'm quite all right," said Professor. But soon Karin had her way, for the old man stumbled and fell. For a moment he lay on his side. Bellissimo stopped and Karin had to push him to make space to kneel down. Before she could kneel, Professor struggled to his knees, to his feet.

"I slipped on a loose stone. It's nothing!" He smiled wryly, rubbing his ankle.

Anxiety had brought a sharp pain to Karin's stomach.

"Please, you mustn't walk another step. You must ride!
Look, Bellissimo's asking you to ride!"

Bellissimo nuzzled Professor nearly off balance. Laughing
and shrugging, the old man let Karin dust him off and
help him onto the donkey's back. He stuffed his feet into
the saddlebags and they set off again, along what had been
a wide shady boulevard, past the huge bombed Kurhaus
to a wooden barracks with a red-and-white flag flying before
it.

And then suddenly it was like arriving home.

The barracks door had opened, letting out a flood of
light. A young man bounded forward, holding out his
hand.

"Welcome! I'm Heinz Schefer. I recognize those ladybird badges. You must be from our beloved Children's
Village!" His handshake nearly brought Professor down
from Bellissimo's back.

Three more young men and two young women came out
of the barracks. They shook hands with Professor and
gathered close to pet Bellissimo and talk to him as if he
were an old friend. They helped Professor down, and one
of them ran for a bucket of water to give the donkey a
drink.

"Come in and have a meal with us," urged Heinz Schefer.
"Stay overnight. We have all that room over there." He
motioned toward the bombed hotel. "We're just setting up
here, arrived only a few weeks ago. We're all Swiss, but
you're no Swiss, you're American. What's an American

doing wandering around Germany with a child and a donkey, so soon after the war?"

"Hurrying out of Germany as fast as I can," replied Professor. The young people laughed.

So he's an American! thought Karin. Professor seemed all at once less an elf, more an ordinary human being. Yet she could understand him no better.

Heinz Schefer led the way to the hotel, up tiers of stone steps, past the tall pillars of the porch and into the foyer, across a mosaic floor, pitted and gouged, past a broken statue where a fountain had played. Above were paintings of cupids—and holes, little breaks in the ceiling, and one huge gaping hole letting in the sky.

They walked with ringing steps along a broad corridor to a room crowded with women and girls knitting and sewing.

"We begin the job of reclothing Aachen," explained the German woman in charge of the workroom. Karin studied faces again, looking for Marianne.

"And can you sew, dear?" asked the German woman.

Karin nodded, blushing with shyness.

Professor said proudly, "For an example of Karin's handiwork, you must examine her donkey's saddlebags!"

That was not difficult to do because Bellissimo had followed Karin into the hotel and was at that moment halfway through the workroom door.

"How lovely! Look, each figure is different! What lovely colors!" came from the group of women and girls who gathered to see the saddlebags.

"You must come help us in the morning," said the German woman. "That is, if you're staying—"

"Of course she's staying," put in Heinz Schefer. "She's to sleep like a princess, in the Gold Room with Anna and Steffi."

After a supper of bread and butter and jam in the barracks, Karin made Bellissimo comfortable in the enclosure behind the hotel, outside the Gold Room, where he could thrust his head through the window. He could see the spoiled plaster modeling on the ceiling, and the pieces of sky showing through, deep purple now and spangled with stars. And he could see the three camp beds, comically small in the huge empty room.

Anna and Steffi were like nurses. They bathed Karin in a tin tub, they cut her nails, they shampooed her hair and rubbed it dry and brushed and combed the snarls from it. They found her a nightgown covered with little flowers, and they brought her a red, woolen cardigan to keep her warm on the journey. They dabbed at the sores on her feet with antiseptic, and wrapped them in bandages. Finally they brought her a drink of hot chocolate and tucked her into bed. She smiled and sighed and thanked them again and again. It was safe here, with Anna and Steffi watching over her.

But she was anxious about Professor and Bellissimo.

"Please—" she began hesitantly. "Do you think we three will get to Switzerland safely? Is it a very long way? And do you think the guards at the border will let Bellissimo cross into Switzerland?"

"Such small shoulders for carrying a weight of cares!" Anna bent over Karin to smooth her hair back from her forehead.

"But please tell me! Do you think it will be all right?" Karin's voice croaked in weariness.

"It will be—all—right, Karin!" said the girls in unison. They grasped her hands, one of them at each side of her bed.

But when they had gone, taking their paraffin lamp with them, Karin turned her head from side to side, listening to the sounds of night in the hotel: the wind picking its way through a thousand gaps and playing tag with loose wall-papers and bits of refuse; the mice, or rats perhaps, scurrying in tap-tapping rushes behind the walls and out into the open of the Gold Room; the scraping of heavy objects; shouts, steps thumping along the corridor, nearer, nearer. . . .

She jumped out of bed and ran to Bellissimo in the window. Delicately he nibbled her cheek, and made a sound in his throat between mewling and whinnying. Hours later Anna and Steffi found her, more asleep than awake, leaning over the sill with her arms around Bellissimo's neck.

Chapter 7

BREAKFAST WAS announced by a chorus of shouts which echoed along the hotel corridors. Karin hurried out to Bellissimo and dashed with him in a big arc around the hotel grounds, coming to a stop at the barracks door.

The others were already seated at the first of the three long trestle tables in the barracks room. Professor called from the head of the table and Karin ran to him and held his arm and beamed into his face—only for an instant. She looked away again because to be growing to love Professor reminded her of her own family, of how she had loved them and of the hurt of their loss.

"Excuse me, I'm sorry I'm late. I was giving Bellissimo his morning run," she said bashfully to no one in particular.

She received a few smiles and nods. She had interrupted the conversation.

Anna was saying, "Those bunker kiddies may have no shoes, but most of them have their mothers still with them."

Heinz grinned at Karin. "Never mind, our Karin shines like a new franc this morning! Smile again for us, Karin!"

Karin hung her head and blushed as she seated herself on the bench beside Professor. Steffi passed her some bread and butter and jam, Anna poured her a cup of coffee, and everybody watched her when Heinz told her:

"This afternoon you and Professor will be driving out of Aachen in a British Red Cross Ambulance, Karin. It's all arranged."

Karin gripped the bench.

"But Belliss—" she cried out.

"With your furry friend aboard as well," Heinz added quickly. "But this morning you must work, all three of you! Can your donkey carry heavy loads?"

"Oh, yes, he's strong and he loves work!" said Karin at once. "But, please, is it a big ambulance? Will there be room for Bellissimo inside?"

"Standing room only," replied Heinz. "Tell him not to try to lie down."

"We'll have to improvise a halter if he's to help with the cement bags," put in the young man named Gerhard.

"He doesn't need a halter. I just tell him what to do," said Karin.

"But you won't be with him. You'll be in the sewing room from nine to eleven, and from eleven to one you'll be helping with the soup," said Heinz.

"Yes, that's all right. First I'll give you a lesson on how to drive him, if you like." She smiled shyly at Gerhard. She was blushing again, yet she felt important. She smiled across at Anna and Steffi, who had brought her clothes, clean and dry and warm, when it was time to get up, and who had drawn over her sore, bandaged feet a fine pair of white socks with tasseled cords to hold them firm below the knee.

Professor rubbed his hands together in pleasure. He wanted to know more about the ambulance, whose ambulance it was, and how far it could carry Karin, Bellissimo and him in the direction of the Swiss border. Heinz took a map from his pocket.

"Eric will be driving the ambulance. He's not one of us, he's a British Quaker. He has to deliver a load of clothing to Frankfurt—here. Here we are, Aachen, and here's how he will travel—about two hundred miles in all—to Cologne and up the Rhine through Bonn and Koblenz. And if he can't find you anywhere to stay when you get to Frankfurt, he's promised to drive you back here again! I don't know why you can't give up the idea of hurrying to Switzerland and stay on with us in any case. We'll find lots for you to do!"

Professor gave a rueful smile.

"I've always had a yen to be a shoemaker," he said, "like my elder brother. He has a shoe factory in New Jersey. But I've made a solemn promise to be in Zurich in four days. There's an important meeting. And immediately after that I must catch my plane to America. Today's Tuesday. We must be in Trogen by Saturday afternoon. Do you think we shall manage it?"

"It's a long journey. But at least you can't get lost. You simply follow the Rhine."

Now Karin was hardly listening. Her brain spun with the facts she had just learned. As soon as they reached the Village Professor would leave her to go to Zurich and then fly back to America. She might never see him again!

Her appetite for breakfast vanished.

Professor drew his finger down the map and raised it as if he had scooped a gold nugget.

"The ambulance will carry us a third of our journey! It's too good to be true! It seems a kind of miracle!" How over-joyed he was, when traveling quickly meant that she would lose him all the sooner!

"It will be time to talk of miracles when you get that don-key over the border and arrive at Trogen unharmed and well," said Heinz. It was clear that he and the others already knew about Bellissimo having no permits.

"Do you think they'll let Bellissimo across?" Karin found courage to ask. She was going to have to lose Professor soon. Would she have to lose Bellissimo, too?

"Nothing's certain in Germany these days," said Heinz.

"But what will happen if they don't let him through?"

"They'll confiscate him."

"Confiscate?"

"That's a polite word for take him away. They might want to put him in quarantine for a few weeks."

"I—I couldn't let them take him away from me," muttered Karin. Everyone noticed that her chin trembled.

Heinz tried to comfort her. "Give those border policemen your new franc smile, Karin, and they'll let you take ten donkeys across!"

Soon there was a scraping of chairs and everybody rushed away, Professor to give Heinz advice on shoemaking, Steffi to the soup kitchen, Anna to the sewing room, the others to dig the foundations for the second barracks.

Karin led Bellissimo to the truck parked on the hotel driveway. The grassy stretch between it and the foundation ditches was soft and uneven, impassable for a truck but ideal for a donkey. Short, square-shouldered Gerhard balanced a bag of cement on Bellissimo's back and followed Karin across the grass for his first lesson in how to drive a donkey without a halter.

"He's a very small donkey," said Gerhard. "You don't think he'll get too tired carrying these heavy bags?"

Bellissimo wrinkled his nose and snorted, as though to say, "Tired? Me?"

Soon Karin left Bellissimo and Gerhard to join Anna in the sewing room. She was put to work cutting out pieces for a set of figures like those on the saddlebags. They would be sewn to a backcloth and used to decorate the sewing room. Steffi let her finish the cuttting before she led her to the barracks to help prepare the midday meal for the old people.

Hundreds of old people crossed the hotel grounds to the barracks at noontime. They waited in a long line, and when Anna opened the door, they streamed inside and seated themselves on the benches round the trestle tables. Anna, Steffi and Karin served the steaming bowls of thick soup and the platefuls of bread. The old people bent over their meal, and for a while there was no talking but only a tinkling and chunking, like the playing of a toy band.

Within an hour the first crowd of old people had left and the second seating had been held. The barracks room grew quiet, but the little kitchen behind it rang with the clatter of dishes and spoons being washed and dried and put away.

Karin helped, hanging up her tea towels as they became wet from the drying. And at almost the same moment that the last dish and spoon were put away, the ambulance arrived.

Heinz came to the barracks to shout the news.

"Eric wants to be off in five minutes. You'd best come out and collect your donkey, Karin. Gerhard has made such a friend of him, he'll howl when he has to give him up!"

Karin hurried out of the kitchen, past the empty tables. She had nearly reached the door when she noticed the little old woman alone in the room, still seated at her place, her hands folded on the table, her face raised expectantly. She was smiling and her head shook gently from side to side. It was Frau Lang, the little old lady who had given her the bell for Bellissimo!

Karin turned back. "Hello! I didn't know you were here. I'm glad to see you again. Bellissimo likes his bell very much."

"And I'm glad to see you," said Frau Lang. "I couldn't believe my eyes when you walked through that door over there. And then if you didn't bring me my soup! I was so pleased I choked on it!"

"I'm sorry I didn't realize it was you," said Karin. Frau Lang waved her hand.

"Oh, there are so many of us. We begin to look alike after a bit." Frau Lang smiled. Her eyes were sad, and her hands trembled and bumped the table.

"I do hope you'll find your daughter and your grand-daughter soon. Do they live very far away?" Karin leaned on the table across from Frau Lang, forgetting for a moment about Bellissimo and the ambulance.

"Very far. In Frankfurt. Too far for me to go to search for them, and there's been no answer to my letters. They went away perhaps. Perhaps they haven't yet come home from the evacuation."

"Frankfurt—" murmured Karin.

"And where do you come from, child?"

"I come from Julich," said Karin softly.

"From Julich! I've heard about Julich! And you—your fam—"

Karin braced herself against the table.

"All were lost," she said in a whisper.

"Your family—all your family?"

Karin nodded. She stood like a wooden doll. Then she shrugged. Outside in the sunshine there were flying steps and the gay laughter of Anna and Steffi, finished with their kitchen work for a few hours.

"Karin! Where are you?" they called.

"She must have gone to the Gold Room," Steffi said. "What a darling she is. I'll hate to see her go."

Two trembling hands closed over Karin's fists on the table edge.

"And that donkey of yours!" said Frau Lang. "The old people were telling me he slept all night with his head stuck through the hotel window and his nose pointing straight at you in your bed!"

Karin whispered good-by and ran out into the sun. On an impulse she stopped and ran back. Frau Lang sat smiling at her thoughts.

"I—I wanted to say," began Karin timidly, "I'm sure you'll get home all right and find your family. You—you mustn't lose hope."

"Hope! I'm crammed full up to the eyes with hope!" cried Frau Lang. "It keeps me alive!" She raised her index finger in the way Professor sometimes did. "Just at this moment I'm hoping for a new family for my young friend, Karin."

"Thank you!" Karin leaned across the table to kiss Frau Lang and ran outside, first to the Gold Room to fetch the saddlebags and her new nightgown, then to Bellissimo and the crowd gathering to watch the departure.

She was in time to see the ambulance rumble along the drive from the hotel and rattle to a stop before the patch of grass where Bellissimo was having a well-earned luncheon. It was a huge square ambulance, painted a dark-khaki color except for a large white circle on its side, with a big red cross inside it. In front it had no doors but only an open compartment. It looked old and rather unsafe.

It was in the back part of the ambulance, between its long narrow seats lined with bales of clothing, that Bellissimo was to be installed. Eric, the driver, a thin-faced young man in a uniform which matched the ambulance, jumped down and hurried to the back, opening both doors. He took off his glasses, screwed up his eyes and held both hands toward Bellissimo, making a measurement of the length of the donkey's legs; then, holding his hands in the same position, he scrambled into the back of the ambulance on knees and elbows, to hold his hands against one of the seats. He jumped down again, grinning.

"It'll just do it, Heinz, old man! Just room, no? It's made for her, it is, yes, it is truly. It gives exactly space for Arabella's fat stomach, is that not so? The bulge comes in just the right place, or rather it will, will it not? Fine!" He put on his glasses again and dry-washed his hands.

"It's not Arabella, it's Bellissimo, and he's a boy donkey," said Steffi.

Heinz steered Eric to Professor and Karin.

"May I present to you Eric. Forgive him for smelling of cod-liver oil. He had a slight accident yesterday."

"Ah, yes, you speak truly, Heinz, old man; yes, absolutely, didn't I?" Eric shook hands with Professor and Karin. "Delighted. Delighted to meet you. It will be a pleasure to have your company, yes. I really mean that. In the fresh air of the cab you won't notice the cod-liver oil very much. I sincerely hope not, indeed!" He took off his glasses again and wiped them vigorously with a khaki handkerchief. "Yes, fine, fine! Excuse me if I must hurry you a bit. I'd like to stop here for a visit but I must ask you to get in, please, if you will, yes, and the donkey, too. I've never transported a donkey, no, never until now. She likes to ride, does she, your Arabella?"

The question was, how to get Bellissimo into the ambulance. There were no steps at the back. Eric explained that he had accidentally knocked them off as he was bringing the ambulance ashore at Ostend. There were no planks to be had to make a ramp, there was not even a ladder.

In the end, Bellissimo was brought closer to the ambulance, Karin was lifted aboard to coax him and keep him calm; and Eric and Heinz stooped down under Bellissimo's stomach. At a signal they each grasped a foreleg and began to raise their shoulders.

Bellissimo squirmed and wriggled and brayed. Shouts of encouragement rose from the crowd.

But at the crucial moment, when Bellissimo's hoofs touched the floor of the ambulance, Eric began to giggle. His shoulders sank lower, his knees wobbled, and his glasses fell to the ground. Bellissimo tilted dangerously and had to be set down.

Eric dusted his glasses and gave his place to Gerhard.

"If we can't get him in," shouted Gerhard to Karin, "can I keep him? After you left us, I marched him along with a bag of cement and then if he didn't insist on doing it all himself. Set off as cool as you please, straight to the spot, and came back and turned around to be loaded! He left me with next to nothing to do!"

Two more volunteers came forward from the crowd, and the lifting began again. Bellissimo was hoisted into the ambulance at last, and though he was indignant and a little frightened, he licked Karin's face and rubbed his sides against the bales of clothing. It promised to be a comfortable and interesting ride.

In the cab there was a box with a cushion for Professor to sit on, and a ledge with a cushion for Karin. Eric climbed to the driver's seat and started the motor.

Heinz made a farewell speech.

"It was very kind of you to help us with the shoe factory, Professor. You've made the whole project come clear!"

"It was a pleasure!" said Professor. "I'll send that stitching machine I was telling you about."

"Wonderful. It's been a privilege to know you—both of you and your educated donkey!" Heinz kept his foot in the ambulance doorway while a carton box of cheese and liverwurst sandwiches and a paper bag holding a bunch of carrots for Bellissimo were handed aboard—and a very important letter on a sheet of crested official paper, brought on the run for Heinz to sign.

Professor read the letter aloud:

"To whom it may concern:

"We of the Don Suisse relief team at work in Aachen hope that you will find it possible to permit the donkey accompanying this child to cross the border into Switzerland.

Heinz Schefer,
Team Leader"

The motor under the stubby hood roared, the horn gave a soft high beep!

"Bless you, Karin," called Steffi and Anna. "Write to us, will you? Just put Steffi and Anna, care of Don Suisse, Aachen."

Karin promised. The world seemed to her to be teeming with kind good people. And there, at the edge of the crowd, was one of the kindest of all, waving and smiling—Frau Lang, who wanted to go back home to Frankfurt.

Frankfurt! Suddenly Karin remembered where she had heard of Frankfurt before. Heinz had pointed to it on the map at breakfast!

"Please—" In her excitement she squeezed Eric's arm tightly. "Please, just one moment. There's a very old lady who wants so badly to go to Frankfurt! She's just there, just over there! I'll run and get her! She can sit here where I'm sitting and I'll sit on the box with Professor!"

She was so breathless she gulped, so eager her eyes were like black marbles.

"Of course, of course, anything, anybody!" Eric's hands flew up from the steering wheel. "We're all here to do a bit of this and that, is it not so, Heinz, old man? Go fetch the old lady, if you please, by all means. Does anyone else want a ride? There's room on top of the bales. And somebody can ride on the donkey!"

Everyone was laughing, turning Karin's earnestness into a joke, a joke shared by tired people with too much work to do. Karin did not mind about the joke. She jumped down and flew to Frau Lang, and came back much more slowly, leading her by the hand. Heinz lifted first Frau Lang, then Karin into the cab. With another beep of the horn, the ambulance set off.

Bellissimo rasped his ears against the metal door jambs and shoved and twisted till he worked his head through the narrow doorway to the front of the ambulance. He pressed his muzzle against Karin's back. He peered over her shoulder to watch the ambulance eat up the hotel drive. He rested his chin on Karin's shoulder. Lights from Professor's prism twinkled in his huge bright eyes, fixed in an expression of astonishment.

Amid cheers and laughter came Heinz's shout, "Take

care of them, Eric! And you, Karin, mind that donkey doesn't chew your ear off!"

The ambulance turned the corner. Still Karin and Professor could see Heinz and the others waving; then they could see only the Swiss flag; and then a broken building hid the Don Suisse settlement from view.

Eric offered around a package of English mints. Frau Lang was crying silently. Professor could not stop smiling, showing the others his joy. But Karin's answering smile hid the thought which came to her now each time she looked at Professor: When we get to Switzerland, he'll go away and I may never see him again.

Chapter 8

IF SHE HAD studied the map that morning at breakfast, Karin would have seen that they were to travel back the way they had come, through Julich. Nearly every bit of the way was the same. Zigzagging around bumps and holes, the ambulance jolted Karin on the seat she shared with Professor. She was afraid that if she didn't hold tight to Professor's arm, he would sway off the seat and out through the open doorway.

And yet, in spite of their having to pick their way along so slowly, they soon passed the place where Karin and Professor had stopped for their picnic. There was the lane along which the roped-together family had come—and there was the barn where she had found Philip, the soldier, where Professor had picked up the gold watch. (She was certain now it was a gold watch.)

They drove into Julich. How white the rubble shone in the afternoon sun! Eric shifted into first gear to get through the openings cut through the ruins.

"Poor little Julich," he said. "Of all the bombed spots I've seen, this is the worst. I've been through here three or four times now, and looked here and there, into the openings and up the hanging staircases and down cellar holes. And I've never seen a soul, not a living soul, I never have."

Karin couldn't bring herself to tell Eric that Julich was her home, that a few months before it had been a pretty place full of families and dogs and cats and nice shops and tidy houses. But Professor and Frau Lang knew, of course, and they took Karin's hands as Eric drove through, pumping his left leg twice on the clutch each time he changed gear. Karin looked straight ahead, and hardly turned her eyes when they passed what was left of her house. But all her efforts weren't enough to swallow the lump in her throat.

"Just as I thought. Not a soul to be seen, not so much as a dog or cat," said Eric as he swung the ambulance round the bend out of Julich.

After a while Karin leaned over Frau Lang so she could see Eric's face.

"I was wondering," she began shyly. "Do you drive about very much?"

"Every day. I'm practically riveted to this old crate," said Eric. "Why?"

"I wondered if you might have seen my friend."

"I see a lot of people. What's your friend's name?"

"Marianne Meister. She's tiny and she has blonde hair and blue eyes—"

"Marianne Meister. I'll remember that name. I'll look out for her. Marianne Meister," said Eric solemnly. "And if I run into her, I'll let you know."

Karin believed he really would. "Oh, thank you very, very

much! I'm going to look for her, too, of course, all along the way."

She was not very hopeful. She had grown used to expecting nothing. So little that was happy or good had happened —until the day before yesterday when Professor found her.

A rush of hope warmed her from head to toe. Now that Professor had found her, perhaps everything would be different!

They passed the lane leading to Globkes' farm. Sitting up high as they were in the cab, Karin and Professor could see all three parts of the farmhouse. They watched for Fräulein Krone, both secretly hoping not to see her.

But there she was, a distance farther along the road, trudging toward Cologne! The suitcase Professor had given her bulged in her right hand; and over her left shoulder she carried a huge sack of potatoes. She set the sack and case down a long time before the ambulance reached her, and thrust out her thumb to beg for a ride.

"It's Karin's old landlady," Professor explained to Eric. "If it's at all possible—"

Eric was not a good driver. He never changed gears without a grinding noise. Now, by the time he could change down and bring the ambulance to a stop, Fräulein Krone and her baggage were a long way behind. She picked up the case and dragged the sack along the road—and stared up into the faces of Professor and Karin.

"You!" was all she said.

"You want to be glad it is them, lady." Eric laughed. "We're loaded to the gunnels as it is. I wouldn't have stopped at all if they hadn't asked me to, isn't that right, Professor? Look here! You made me stop. You can have the job of stowing the lady. Ask her if she likes donkeys."

Karin and Professor offered to go into the back with Bellissimo. Bales were stacked higher and a place was found for Fräulein Krone's sack of potatoes. Space was cleared at the end of each seat, by the back door, for Karin and Professor. Fräulein Krone insisted on keeping the suitcase in front with her. She seated herself bolt upright, the case rubbing against her knees, and against Frau Lang's, and getting in Eric's way.

Bellissimo sniffed at Fräulein Krone, flattened his ears and drew his head back in through the narrow doorway. By laying a cheek on one of the bales, he could see a piece of Karin out of the corner of his eye. He stayed in that position all the way to Cologne.

Once inside the city, Eric grew more and more impatient with Fräulein Krone. He revved the motor, jabbed on his brake pedal, and gave everyone a bumpy ride up and down the bombed streets, following her directions. His face grew red and shiny. Twice the way was blocked by debris and he had to back and turn the ambulance. The rubble with the sun on it dazzled him. There seemed to be no smooth bit of road in the whole of Cologne.

"To the right, to the left, around the church and straight ahead!" shouted Eric above the bumping and rasping and roaring of the ambulance. "Ask anybody how to get anywhere in Germany these days and it's always To the right, to the left, around the church and straight ahead! And you end up where you started from!"

Finally they drew up before the shabby house where Fräulein Krone's sister lived. Karin and Professor, climbing out of the back of the ambulance and hauling the potatoes out after them, heard Fräulein Krone address her sister crossly:

"Well, you don't seem pleased to see me! And after all I've been through!"

There was a quick shaking of hands all around, because anything less than that would have been exceedingly rude, and Karin and Professor climbed to their old seat, with a warm smile for Frau Lang. Professor couldn't resist calling after Fräulein Krone:

"How nice it is to know that you've had no need of the donkey after all!"

The house door slammed shut.

"They could have invited us in for a coffee." Eric shrugged. "But never mind. I've a few chocolates here. She got the box out of her suitcase. What a box! And I took enough for all of us." He held the chocolates out. He had used his diary for a plate. He popped one into his mouth.

"Mmm," he mumbled, "they're as good as English chocolates!"

"They're better, they're American!" said Professor, and he and Karin laughed.

After Cologne was left behind, the road surface improved and Eric drove faster. Bellissimo, with his head back inside the cab, seemed to think he was on the road himself, running at top speed. He stretched his neck and opened his mouth. The wind ruffled his fur and blew his thick lashes back. He narrowed his eyes and snorted excitedly.

Now for the first time they were following the River

Rhine. The road and the river were twin cords threading
through fields and villages and hamlets, keeping as close to
one another as they could. Sometimes a forest or a mountain would drive the road overland; but soon it would press
its way back, as if it adored to be near the wide glossy water.

At five o'clock Eric drove off the road and came to a stop
in a meadow. He jumped down from the cab.

"Time for tea!" he announced, hurrying round to help the
others down.

Bellissimo was coaxed out onto a stairway of clothing
bales.

"Let's hope he'll get back in as willingly," said Eric. "If
he won't, we'll have to ship him downriver on a raft, that's
all."

Bellissimo ran wild! He dashed into the meadow as if he
would trample flat every primrose, every blade of grass. He
threw his head high and brayed loudly and hoarsely, "Eee-
awr! Eee-awr!" He rolled onto his back and thrashed his
legs in the air.

The travelers settled themselves on the tarpaulin from the
back of the ambulance, and gazed around. They were four
small specks on a plateau among mountains which pushed
so close that the river had to spend all her force carving
a way through. She dug deeper as she went, thrusting and
battering against the rocks until she changed from a twinkling dancer to a hag who growled and grumbled and
threatened.

But she could not spoil the picnic. Eric was an excellent
tea-maker. He brought out a large square tin, a small spirit

stove and a blackened kettle filled with water. Under a back seat of the ambulance he found four tea-stained pint mugs; and within five minutes he and his passengers sat among the buttercups and daisies, eating sandwiches and sipping tea.

"We've found a bright new meadow,
Where the grass is green and sweet.
We've big pint mugs of tea to drink,
And sandwiches to eat!"

sang Professor. Everyone, even Frau Lang, helped him sing the rhyme the next time through.

"I must take you back to Aachen," said Eric, "as our team jester."

"And must I, too, take my baths in cod-liver oil?" Professor chuckled.

In the warm sunshine Eric did smell strongly. Karin noticed that his trousers were covered with greasy stains.

"Yes, by all means!" Eric laughed. "We indulge in cod-liver-oil showers. We stand under the barrel and take the bung out, glunk, glunk, glunk!" He went on in quieter tones. "The worst of it is I have no other clothes, no, not a rag, will you believe it? I'll have to drag around like a stranded fish for another fourteen months. How about making me a pair of trousers out of those very handsome saddle-bags, Karin? I could put on a turban and be a visiting potentate, could I not?"

Karin knew Eric was joking. He was smiling at her expectantly. Her chance had come to ask him the question she carried with her as closely as Professor carried his prism.

"Do you think they'll let him in?"

"Let who in where?"

"Bellissimo—into Switzerland. We have no permits for him, you see, only the letter from Heinz Schefer."

From his breast pocket Eric drew a card. On it was a large red-and-black star and words Karin could not read from where she sat. Eric turned the card over and wrote in English:

The Friends Ambulance Team at work in Aachen urge that the donkey accompanying this child be allowed to cross into Switzerland.

Eric signed his name, handed the card to Karin, cleaned his glasses and stood up.

"If you please, one and all, we'd best not arrive too late at Frankfurt. It's time we got aboard. Karin, you may direct the donkey operations, if you like."

It had not been difficult to coax Bellissimo out of the ambulance, but it was impossible to coax him in again. He came to Karin readily enough and she pushed him and pulled him, whispered in his ear and stood inside the ambulance dangling the bunch of carrots the Don Suisse team had donated. But Bellissimo baulked. Ten minutes went by. Karin sank into despair. It was more than a hundred miles to Frankfurt; and when they reached there they must take Frau Lang home and then find somewhere to sleep themselves. She and Professor had better tell Eric and Frau Lang to drive on. They themselves would have to do the rest of the journey on foot.

But Professor would grow too tired again.

To make matters worse, it began to rain, with the sun still shining and a rainbow spanning the river. Professor opened his umbrella. As he brought it toward Karin, there was a darting flash over the grass. A light brushed Karin's face and she rubbed her eyes. Was it lightning or was it a magic ray from the prism?

As Professor held the umbrella over Karin and looked about for Frau Lang to shelter her, too, he heard the singing.

Pushing Bellissimo once more, leaning against his rear and shoving with her hands, with her head, pushing with all her energy and will, too disappointed to plead with the donkey any longer, Karin heard the singing.

Eric, stuffing his tea-making equipment away, heard it. All three straightened their backs and gazed across the field. Bellissimo pricked his ears, gave a little jump, and dashed away.

From the road came a party of boys, captained by Frau Lang. The biggest of the boys shouted orders above the singing. The company was supposed to march in good order. But the pace was too slow and the boys turned cartwheels and played leapfrog as they came across the meadow. Karin counted ten of them, most of them dressed in leather trousers, all wearing wooden-soled sandals like her own, all carrying empty knapsacks on their backs.

"You were so busy," explained Frau Lang breathlessly as she delivered the boys, "and I had nothing to do so I went for help!"

"And as it happens, there's not a thing we'd enjoy doing

more than lifting a donkey into an ambulance!" The big boy laughed. "Come on, fellows, off with the packs."

Ten knapsacks fell to the grass.

"Now fan out and close in on him!" came the next order. "Get in there and grab him! Hey, Ferdi, come back here!"

Ferdi was one of the smaller boys. With a wide grin he raced ahead, not slackening his pace for anyone but holding both arms out forward as he neared Bellissimo.

The other boys followed like beaters.

Bellissimo had gone through a gate and was idly cropping grass in a second meadow farther from the river. He seemed to the boys an indifferent, lazy donkey. He did not even bother to glance at Ferdi as he drew near.

But suddenly, when Ferdi was almost upon him, Bellissimo braced himself, head up, ears pricked, nostrils distended. With a few graceful prances he by-passed Ferdi and the other boys and galloped off. He made a wide circle around the meadow's edge. Karin called him and he thundered toward her, but instead of halting he galloped by, tossing his head.

"He wants to play tag!" Karin shouted to the boys. She gazed back forlornly at Professor, Eric and Frau Lang, waiting by the ambulance. Running up behind the boys, Karin said, "We used to play tag with him at home, you see. When he saw you he remembered. He's there—look at him—waiting for us to chase him."

"Well, what are we waiting for?" shouted Ferdi. He and the others rushed toward Bellissimo. They capered on the way, hauling at one another's suspenders, smacking one another, hooting and calling one another by nickname. Again Ferdi was ahead. Straight at Bellissimo he ran. There before him was the donkey, shaking his ears, blowing through his nostrils. But in a twinkling he was off—a circus horse trotting and cantering and galloping around the ring.

Breathing heavily, the boys leaned against a fence—all but Ferdi, who would not give up. He shouted to Karin each time he rushed by, "When I catch him can I have a ride?"

Eric and Professor brought the remainder of the sandwiches to the boys. They sprawled against the fence, or climbed onto it, eating with big bites, talking as they chewed. Eric and Professor went back to Frau Lang, waiting by the ambulance.

At first nobody noticed Bellissimo trotting across the meadow with Ferdi on his back. Donkey and boy didn't stop as they came toward the fence, but veered, cantering past the boys and out into the meadow again.

Nine boys shouted at once.

"I didn't see him catch that donkey, did you?"

"How'd you get on, Ferdi?"

"Did he buck you?"

"Good old Ferdi, he's all right! Stick it, Ferdi!"

"He's got guts, has Ferdi!"

"Hey, Ferdi, how're you going to stop?"

"Neither of them looks like wanting to stop!"

Gripping with his knees, chin raised, laughing loudly, Ferdi urged Bellissimo on, as if riding a donkey were the one thing he'd had his heart set on doing since as far back as he could remember.

Karin drew out the carrots again and ran into Bellissimo's path. The donkey side-stepped with a saucy shake of his ears. It was only when Ferdi and Bellissimo decided between themselves to stop and walked sedately toward the ambulance that the boys were able to sweep in and lift him by his four legs and his middle, with Ferdi still on his back, and deposit him between the ambulance seats. Hurriedly Eric shut the doors.

"Thank you one and all!" He beamed, dry-washing his hands.

"No thanks needed. It was a lark!" The boys helped one another with their knapsacks. They picked up the extra one, and two of them climbed into the front of the ambulance to haul Ferdi off Bellissimo's back.

"He's nuts about animals. He used to live on a farm," they explained.

Karin saw the joy in Ferdi's face when he said:

"I spoke soft to him and he let me get on his back! He likes me! Look, he's sticking his head through the door!"

Ferdi would have gone back to Bellissimo if the others hadn't dragged him away. They tramped obliquely across the meadow, in order to meet the road farther along. Every few steps one or the other of them turned to wave, Ferdi oftenest of all.

"Where are you heading? Are you out hiking for pleasure?" Eric called after them.

"No—for potatoes!" They thumped their knapsacks. "Five or ten miles into the country. We've an alarm clock and a few cigarettes and— Got any potatoes?"

"No, but wait a minute! Just up there at the edge of the road," shouted Eric. He and his passengers climbed into the ambulance and bumped their way across the meadow, following the boys.

"I was just going to say," said Eric, when he had lurched over the bumpy verge and onto the road, "there's not much room left but hop in and we'll help you along a few miles."

There was room enough. Two boys sat in each empty square at the back of the ambulance, two lay on top of the clothing bales, five hung onto the front, half in and half out. Ferdi had the honor of riding on Bellissimo again. He lay with his cheek against the donkey's neck, and stroked and scratched the backs of his ears, and whispered, "Funny old donkey! Funny old boy!"

Twenty minutes later, Eric set the boys down.

"Thanks a million! Now we'll be home before dark, and we've come farther than ever before!" The boys shook hands all around and separated Ferdi from Bellissimo again. They waited at the side of the road to wave.

"A fine journey for all of you, with good luck at the end of it!"

Karin saw, leaning out of the ambulance to wave, that Ferdi stood aside from the others, squeezing his face between his fists to keep himself from crying.

Chapter 9

IT WAS DARK when they reached Frankfurt. The city was so changed that until they came close to the first church spire, Frau Lang could not believe she was home. She sat on the edge of her seat, her forehead almost rubbing the windshield of the ambulance. She gave little exclamations as she recognized in the glow of the headlights this house, that corner, this bit of park— But her exclamations turned to gasps for Frankfurt was little better than Aachen or Cologne or Julich.

Part way along a road that looped in and out of rubble, Eric felt a trembling against his arm and knew he was to stop the ambulance. Karin and Professor helped Frau Lang down. Eric turned the ambulance so its headlights made a path for her and she could find her way to the rubbish heap that had been her house. She picked up a board and stumbled about, stopping every few steps to dig down a little with the board. She wandered aimlessly, as if half asleep.

Karin and Professor climbed back into the ambulance and sat looking ahead at nothing. Eric said:

"What shall we do with her? Should we leave her? I could come for her when I turn back toward Aachen. She might find somebody who knows what's become of her family. But

I can't just drive off and leave her. Where would she sleep? And it wouldn't be safe, not a bit. She'd be sure to fall in the dark or cut herself or bump her head or wander off or any one of a million things—"

Karin thought, If Eric takes Frau Lang back to Aachen, back to that hole in the alley, she'll just curl up and die!

Frau Lang returned and they helped her up to her seat in the ambulance. No one said a word to her. Karin laid her hand softly against a trembling shoulder.

They drove deeper into Frankfurt. They were lost in thought and, at first, did not notice the figure in the road ahead. Eric jabbed on the brake with such force that his passengers toppled from their seats.

It was a disheveled woman in a torn dress. Her face was twisted in shock and fear.

"My son—hospital—quick! A mine went off! He's hurt! You understand? He's—over there!" She pointed into the darkness.

"Stay where you are, Karin. Take care of Frau Lang." Professor was abrupt and stern. He jumped from the ambulance. He was the first to open the back doors, to draw out one of the stretchers lying ready under the seats. He and Eric followed the woman into the darkness, down a gully between two houses whose outlines Karin could see dimly against the sky. Their feet scrunched over cement and stones. They had no light, and soon the night swallowed them up.

Karin let herself down into the road. She stood in the glow of the ambulance lights, and watched and listened. Her eyes were trained on the dip between the buildings; her ears heard only the faint whistle of the wind.

It flashed upon her that Professor was in terrible danger, that there might be a second mine near the first. A wild urge to save him sent her hurrying over the rubble. You could step on a mine, anywhere, in a wood, on a grass verge, tucked against the edge of a road or path.

Where the ground began to fall away between the houses, she stopped, her arms wrapped tightly across her chest, her hands pressing her shoulders. Perspiration rose on her temples. To go farther meant disobeying Professor. He wanted her to stay in the ambulance with Frau Lang.

She turned back, pausing every few steps to listen. She crept back into the cab and knelt on the floor, her face against the windshield. Bellissimo gave his bell a shake, to tell her he was glad she was nearer.

They brought the boy on the stretcher and laid him on one of the rows of clothing bales in the back of the ambulance. Professor rode in back to hold him still, while the mother crowded into the front to show Eric the way to the hospital. Grim-faced, trembling so that he had more trouble than usual with his gears, Eric drove into the heart of Frankfurt. Karin, squeezed close to him now that she shared the center seat with Frau Lang, noticed the whiteness of his knuckles on the wheel. It was important to go gently, but it was more important to hurry. The ambulance worked its way through the city clumsily, swaying and bumping. The boy's mother gave directions in a high, quaking voice. Endlessly she clenched and unclenched her fingers. Karin stole a glance at her face, and looked quickly away.

They drew to a stop before a high gateway. A sleepy caretaker shambled from the gatehouse, shading his eyes from the glare of the headlights with one hand as he fumbled with the catch. There was a delay while he kicked and shoved one of the gates which stuck on a rise of ground. The ambulance rumbled along a curving drive to the main entrance of the hospital.

Eric jumped down and ran into the brightly lit hall. They heard his voice. Two men in white ran out to the ambulance and carried the stretcher swiftly into the hospital. Karin made a single daring effort to see the boy's face. It seemed to her beautiful, like a doll's face against the light-green stretcher.

Again Karin, Frau Lang and Bellissimo were left in the ambulance. There was nothing to do but wait. It comforted Karin to be close to Frau Lang, to notice how calm and still the old lady had become. Her head no longer shook from side to side as it had when she had come back from the ruins of her house. She sat with hands clasped, her fingertips touching her chin. It seemed as if she could go on patiently waiting forever.

Presently Karin noticed that Frau Lang's lips were moving, that she held her eyes closed and smiled gently. She was praying, Karin knew, not for herself but for the boy.

An hour went by. Without hearing a word, Karin was drawn into Frau Lang's prayers. It seemed the "Amen" when Eric came striding toward the ambulance.

"He's going to be all right! They've given him a transfusion and he's going to be all right!" Eric was grinning broadly. It was a wonder that so many large teeth could fit between his jaws. He couldn't keep his hands and feet still.

He rocked on his heels and kicked at the tires of the ambulance. He clamped and rubbed his hands together and rumpled and smoothed his hair. "It's the greatest thing that's happened since I was born," he said, "absolutely the greatest. It is truly!"

He set about making tea then and there on the hospital grounds, and no one came to complain. Everybody drank a mugful, Professor, Karin, Frau Lang, and the boy's mother —Eric himself drank three. Still confined to the ambulance, Bellissimo ate the bunch of carrots which he had not earned before. When Karin held them out he nuzzled and sniffed them, then took them into his mouth gingerly, one after the other. Thoughtfully he crunched them, keeping them in his mouth and sucking as the twins had sucked the chocolate. Lastly he ate the paper bag which had held them.

Professor sat clasping his knees and smiling at everyone. Karin had seen him happy like this once before: when he had told her how pleased he was to find her. This time she noticed something new about him. His eyebrows took turns leaping up and bobbing as he spoke. And she noticed something now very familiar: Reflecting the lights from the hospital, the prism shone and twinkled as if it, too, wanted to tell its happiness. Karin gazed at it wonderingly. Was it magic, did it give Professor power to make things come right? How lovingly he was turning it in his fingers at this very moment. Could it be helping them to find their way safely to Switzerland, was it a charm that could help everyone in its path?

Frau Maggold, the boy's mother, turned out to be a jolly,

roly-poly woman. Now that her horror had changed to joy she kept taking deep breaths and laughing and making little exclamations, "Ah!" and "Wonderful!" and "Not to be believed!" She could not thank Eric enough. Over and over again she told him how grateful she was. All at once she swooped down on Professor to squeeze both his shoulders in her pudgy hands.

"You are no ordinary old man, you are an angel dropped from Heaven, I'll stake my life on it! Nothing, nothing is too good for you, nothing is too much to do." She threw out her arms and lifted her voice as if to invite the whole hospital. "I shall take you home with me, that's what I shall do, all of you! I shall send for my friend to come make her famous applecake, and I shall draw water for baths, and bring out my best linen sheets I haven't used since before the war, and we shall sit down to such a meal, such a meal! And even then I won't have thanked you half enough!"

Eric stowed his tea-making equipment, and the ambulance rolled away past the sleepy watchman at the gate, through Frankfurt and along the Hanau road, turning down a bumpy cart track to a large modern brick farmhouse. Frau Maggold's guests filed indoors and sat like waiting patients on the hard chairs in the parlor. One by one they were called upstairs for their baths. Four farm cats entered the room and formed a semi-circle around Eric. Lynx-eyed, purring, they sniffed his aroma of cod-liver oil.

Karin left her chair repeatedly to try to calm Bellissimo. Outside the parlor window he was calling her in a dirge of rasping "eea's" which threatened to unsettle every animal on the farm. Frau Maggold thrust her head through the parlor doorway.

"Your donkey can't be wanting a bath, too, can he? If he knows what's good for him he'll follow us to the barn. Come, Karin, I'll lead the way."

Bellissimo was shown into the largest and airiest stall in the barn. Soon a hay bag hung a few inches from his nose, oats and bran mash, chaff and water waited in separate troughs. In a box in the corner of his stall lay samples of his favorite food in all the world, beets.

Karin scratched behind his ears.

"You've had a tremendous ride, Bellissimo, and you didn't once complain. Now, you see, you've been crowned Prince of Donkeys! Come on and laugh for me!"

Bellissimo shook his head.

"You won't? With all this lovely food to eat you won't laugh?"

Karin sighed, kissed her donkey and left him to his banquet, to be followed by a blissful sleep in which his ears twitched, in which he brayed softly, dreaming of oats and bran and chaff and field after field of his favorite beets.

Karin returned to the parlor and sat listening to the sounds of the house. Frau Maggold seemed to be everywhere at once, clattering plates in the dining room, carrying water upstairs for the baths, making up the guest beds, banging in the kitchen, bustling into the parlor with cups of coffee and biscuits to tide her guests over till supper was ready.

"And now—" Frau Maggold stood, arms akimbo, beaming in the parlor door. "Now we'll move across the hall for our meal. My friend has made a huge applecake, and there's fresh cream. We don't live on a farm for nothing!"

Over her shoulder she called, "Trude! Come and join us now, Trude!"

The dining room was warm and cheery after the mustiness of the parlor. Candlelight glowed over the table, over the gay flower centerpiece and the plates of smoked meats and cheeses and cakes and biscuits. A young woman entered from the kitchen, carrying the steaming cake. She was laughing out loud, and her face was red from her baking.

"Just put it here, Trude. Everybody find a seat. You, dear old man"—Frau Maggold took possession of Professor again —"must be the guest of honor and sit at the head of the table! Trude, come, I must introduce you!"

Frau Lang, shining and smiling since her bath, wearing the flowered dress Frau Maggold had insisted on giving her, had come into the dining room like a queen, holding Karin's arm. But suddenly, halfway across the room, Karin felt a jolt against her and turned to see her aged friend fall sideways to the floor.

"Frau Lang! What's wrong?" gasped Karin. "Oh, Professor, she's fainted!"

Everyone whirled around. Frau Maggold was the first to reach the old woman, to lift her head from the floor.

"Go for water!" she shouted.

But Trude rushed forward, pushing everyone aside. She knelt on the floor and took Frau Lang into her arms. She gazed up at Frau Maggold.

"It's—my—mother!" she whispered. Then she sobbed it, louder and louder, "It's Mother! It's Mother!"

Rocking Frau Lang like a baby, she wept uncontrollably as if she could never stop.

"Mother! Mother! We've looked everywhere for you! We've been to Aachen six times. We've searched everywhere, even through all the bunkers! We were going to try just once more! We nearly gave up hope! Oh, run for my daughter, somebody! Hurry! Oh, Mother, Mother, open your eyes!"

Trude stopped her rocking and gazed at Professor imploringly. "She's all right, sir? She's going to be all right?"

Professor went down on his knees, too, to feel Frau Lang's pulse. Frau Maggold brought a bowl of water and rushed away to find Trude's daughter. Frau Lang opened her eyes and smiled ecstatically.

Soon she was seated at the table with her daughter on one side, her granddaughter on the other. Karin saw such rejoicing as she had never in her life seen before.

Chapter 10

THE NEXT morning was caught up in good-bys. First there was the parting from Frau Lang. Frau Maggold and Eric were already seated in the ambulance, Frau Maggold eager to see her son again, Eric anxious to deliver the bales of clothing and begin the journey back to Aachen.

And Bellissimo was aboard. Frau Maggold had dragged out the ramp she used in transporting cattle, and with four people pushing from behind, Bellissimo had skidded up the ramp and into the ambulance as neatly as if he were one of Eric's bales.

Frau Lang held Karin's face in her hands and kissed her. She gazed earnestly at Professor.

"Take care of her," she said. "She's brought the sun out for me and driven all the shadows away. My life has begun again—all because of Karin!"

Frau Lang stood in the cart tracks waving her handkerchief until the ambulance was lost from view. The last glimpse they had of her she had linked arms with her daughter and granddaughter and turned back to the house.

At the hospital gates there was the parting from Frau Maggold. She worked Professor's right arm up and down as she would the pump handle in her yard.

"I shall always believe you were sent from Heaven," she said. "You and the good Eric have saved my boy's life and I shall never forget either of you. I don't like to let you go on —an old man and a little girl and a donkey. It's too hard, too far. If the weather should turn bad—I lay awake half the night worrying about you and making plans for you. I have an aunt at St. Raphael's Hospital near Schulheim. That's directly on your route. It's about fourteen miles from Mainz. I've written my aunt about you. You must stop at her hospital and give her this letter and she will help you. She will put two hot water bottles in each of your beds when she reads this letter! But you must promise this: Promise you will come back to me if anything goes wrong. I'll take care of you for a year, ten years, gladly! The name of the hospital is on the envelope. Sister Agnes—that's my aunt. Ask for her at once."

Then Frau Maggold shook hands with Eric.

"You're a bit of an angel, too," she chuckled, "you with your bumpy chariot. You'll be welcome at my farm whenever you come to Frankfurt. Bring all your friends!"

She threw her arms around Professor, then around Karin, kissing them each on both cheeks. She gave Professor's shoulders a little shake, sighed heavily and bustled away down the hospital drive.

Karin and Professor climbed back into the ambulance to go with Eric to deliver the clothing bales, then back the way they had come as far as Mainz. Once again there was the problem of getting Bellissimo out of the ambulance. But he hadn't enjoyed riding without the bales, bumping against the hard seats. With help from two young men who were passing, Bellissimo reached the ground in a swing and a thump.

Eric shook hands with Karin and Professor and tugged at Bellissimo's forelock.

"I'd like to go all the way to Switzerland with you three, I would that," he said. "I like adventure. When I get back to Aachen and tell them what happened to us yesterday, they'll think I've made it all up out of second-hand clothing! Well— Write me, won't you, Karin? I'll be looking out for Marianne Meister. Oh, by the way, how do you like my new trousers? Natty, don't you think? Frau Maggold gave them to me. They're not a bad match."

They were much too big. They gave Eric's bouncy walk a clownish touch. Karin and Professor tried not to laugh at him as he climbed aboard and drove off with a scraping of gears and a long shrill Beeeep! of the horn. He leaned out to wave. The sun flashed on his glasses. Too soon the ambulance disappeared.

They themselves walked southward. The river was far below now, still battling against the Taunus Mountains. When the mountains pressed close, the Rhine gathered her strength and hurled herself through narrow passages, sometimes swelling and cascading, sometimes bending sharply, but always winning through and dashing free.

Time was growing short. In three days Professor must be in Zurich to catch his plane. They had come a long way, but they must travel two hundred miles to reach the Swiss border; and after that there would be the train trip to Trogen.

Karin gazed down the road as far as she could see. It was impossible, they could never do it in time. Without a miracle, a whole procession of miracles— Her gaze slid round Bellissimo to Professor.

Frau Maggold had thrown Karin's wooden-soled sandals away in disgust. Today Karin wore a pair of walking shoes, the pair the injured boy had grown out of recently. They were strong and shiny. They had had to be stuffed with rags to keep them from coming off at each step, but it no longer hurt to walk. Bellissimo's saddlebags were full of good things to eat, home-made maize bread, and cheese, even some applecake left over from last night. And in Professor's pocket was the note to Frau Maggold's aunt.

Karin made calculations as she walked along. The hospital was fourteen miles from Mainz. They could walk a mile in about twenty minutes. In six or seven hours, taking time to stop along the way, they should be there.

But fourteen miles was surely too far for an old man to walk. She must watch Professor closely. She must notice when his breath came quicker, when his heels dragged as they had in Aachen two days before. This time she would stop and refuse to budge till he climbed on Bellissimo's back.

Bellissimo stepped along in his twinkle-hoofed gait as if he would never be tired again. He tossed his head, he jolted his bags and rang his bell. His ears stood up like spires. The world belonged to him today. The sunshine, the crisp air, the scent of blossoms, the smells of roadside farms—all were his. Going over the brow of a hill, he brayed, claiming the sky and the clouds for his, and every bird. He came down into a bombed hamlet, and children playing among the rubble rushed closer to stare at him.

"Look, a donkey!" they cried.

"It's a donkey!"

"It's a real live donkey!"

They followed Bellissimo, shouting and laughing. Bellissimo brayed again, and forgot to stay behind Karin.

> "Come one, come all, I'll set the pace,
> We'll have a jolly donkey race!"

His brays said it, and the toss of his head and the clomp of his hoofs. Karin had to run to catch up to him and yank his tail tuft to remind him he was going too fast.

Soon they were in the country again. Professor pointed to a flock of birds coasting down the sky.

"On their way to Switzerland!" He swept the air with his umbrella, which he was using as a walking stick. "The birds fly that way, the stars move that way, donkeys and all intelligent people walk that way—"

"And a tired old monk— Can he come, too?" a voice flashed out at them. Professor and Karin stopped short. Seated on a hill under a cherry tree, fanning himself with a fistful of leaves, was a man in a long black robe. He raised himself with a rustling and jangling. Standing he was tremendous. The yards and yards of cloth it took to cover him swung and billowed around him in the breeze. Smiling gaily, stretching out his hand, he came down the hill.

"Brother Christopher," he said, "worn, tired, hot and footsore."

"An old professor beyond his usefulness, a child at the beginning of hers, and a most useful beast of burden," said Professor. "All three perky as lambs and pleased to meet you! Will you join us for lunch?"

"Thank you!" Brother Christopher bowed. "As you see, I've already reserved a table." Karin's eyes followed Brother Christopher's gesture to the cherry tree. In its shade lay a small leather suitcase, a broad-brimmed black hat and a white handkerchief, spread out like a miniature tablecloth.

"I'm sorry I had no warning of your coming," said Brother Christopher, "and am unable to provide iced water."

"Not to worry," said Professor. "In the donkey's saddlebags we have two bottles of milk, fresh this morning. You will join us in a glass?"

"Thank you, I shall be delighted!" Brother Christopher helped to unbuckle Bellissimo's load. Then he raised Bellissimo's chin and gazed into his huge, limpid, brown eyes.

"I have met a number of donkeys in my life," he said, "black, gray and white, fat and thin, straight and curly, but I have never met a handsomer donkey, a better-groomed and cared-for and kindlier donkey than you! I am pleased to make your acquaintance!" Still holding Bellissimo's muzzle in the palm of one hand, he reached out with the other to scratch behind the twitching, waggling ears. Karin thought for a moment Bellissimo was going to laugh. She herself could not look at Brother Christopher without laughing inside.

Bellissimo cantered into the field, and Brother Christopher invited Karin and Professor to be seated round the handkerchief table. All three helped to make the sandwiches. The talk was in German, so Karin could understand.

"And what is a monk doing wandering along a lonely road in Germany a few months after the war?" asked Professor.

"Oh, you meet all sorts of odd creatures wandering about after a war—" Brother Christopher's hand flew to his mouth. He thumped his knee. "What am I saying? You, my friend, you are no odd one, you are a trusty knight in hat and gloves, his faithful umbrella in hand, his charger close by—and his lovely princess at his side. You have rescued her from a fiery dragon."

The thought of Fräulein Krone as a fiery dragon set Karin and Professor back on their elbows laughing. Brother Christopher watched them quizzically, his arms on his knees. His bare toes peeped out from the straps of his sandals, not wooden-soled sandals, Karin noticed, but soft brown ones of the same leather as his suitcase. He broke his sandwich into two and held the pieces politely. His nails were large and pink, the color of the cherry blossoms which drifted down to rest on his shoulders and along his wide sleeves.

"You are on your way to Switzerland," said Brother Christopher. "I recognize the ladybird badges. I've heard about the Children's Village. You have a long way to go."

"We want to be there in three days. Professor has to catch a plane," said Karin, trying not to show her dread of the parting.

"You'll need wings yourselves to do it," said Brother Christopher. "Maybe you could manufacture some by waving that prism about. I've never seen a prism like that. It's like sitting under a rainbow. But wings or no wings, you'll need somewhere to sleep tonight. You must come along with me, I know just the spot. Six miles farther along this road we come to—"

"St. Raphael's Hospital!" joined in Professor.

They laughed again, all three. It turned out that Brother Christopher was on his way to help celebrate the hospital's hundreth anniversary.

"It's not to begin till evening," he said. "We should be there in time. We shall be delighted to have you at the celebration."

They finished their meal, called Bellissimo, and strapped on the saddlebags. Brother Christopher shook out his handkerchief and put on his hat.

"You've only one small case. What a pity," said Karin.

"Why a pity?" asked Brother Christopher.

"It's a pity because Bellissimo does so like to make himself useful. He notices when something is put into his bags. It makes him feel important. But he likes things put into both bags. He won't be satisfied with one small case."

Brother Christopher beamed.

"Excuse me one moment. Just walk along. I'll catch up to you."

He disappeared behind a hedge. Soon he scurried up behind, carrying in each hand a long thin case made of pillow ticking. At the top of each case was a large safety pin.

"Two hundred and fifty bars of chocolate, a hundred and twenty-five in each case," he announced. "They've gone somewhat soft in sun and heat, but half an hour in the hospital cellars will starch them up again. They're for the children. Brought them all the way from Philadelphia."

Brother Christopher deposited a case in each of Bellissimo's saddlebags. Stiff with their stacks of bars, the cases stuck up like two striped trouser legs; the top parts where the pins were flopped over like feet.

"He's a circus donkey with a clown riding on him upside down!" exclaimed Karin.

They walked three abreast, Karin in the middle. Bellissimo came along behind, sometimes nudging Karin or breathing down her neck. Karin asked Brother Christopher:

"You've traveled such a long way. I wonder if you might have seen my friend. Her name is Marianne Meister."

"And does she have a smile like Karin's?" asked Brother Christopher.

It was useless asking people if they'd seen Marianne. How could they be expected to remember one small blonde girl out of the millions of children in Germany?

With the hiss and roar of the river to accompany him, Professor made up another poem as they walked along.

"You'll never guess what I saw,
I'm sure it's against the law!
Two trouser legs and stocking feet,
Upside down on a donkey's seat,
Waving around in the noonday heat,
And the donkey, he said 'Hee-haw! Hee-haw!'
And the donkey, he said 'Hee-haw!'"

"Say it again!" urged Karin.

Professor recited his poem a second time.

"Do you know," said Karin hesitantly, "I think that will fit the tune we made up before—if we just add a bit."

"It will? Let's hum it then!" Professor seemed to have quite forgotten the tune. Karin had to correct him in every phrase. But soon it came right, and they taught it to Brother Christopher, who harmonized in a huge bass voice.

Brother Christopher said, "And by some remarkable co-incidence that tune exactly fits my road teaser!" He waited for Professor to ask:

"And what, my dear young man, is a road teaser?"

"I'll show you." Brother Christopher began the song again, and as he sang he proceeded not exactly to dance and not exactly to march but to move forward in a combination of heel pointing, toe pointing, leg sweeping and stamps.

He taught his road teaser to the others and they formed a trio, arms linked. They set the steps to the song. They sang loudly and clearly, and soon there was no need to watch their feet. They knew the routine and kept perfect time. They bobbed along almost as quickly as they had walked before.

"And now for my variations!" said Brother Christopher. He pulled loose from his troupe and darted forward with a run and a leap, throwing out his arms so the breeze billowed his sleeves and his skirts. He came to a stop a distance down the road with an improvisation: a pirouette, an arabesque and three hard stamps.

Karin and Professor hooted in glee.

But what had come over Bellissimo? He plunged through the gap left by Brother Christopher. He shook his ears, he rang his bell, he reared and brayed and minced down the road, not trotting or cantering but dancing! Bellissimo was surely dancing! And when he reached Brother Christopher he wheeled to face Karin and Professor.

Suddenly he rolled up his lip, tossed his head, opened his mouth and gave a rasping, rolling, husky snicker. Again and again he snickered.

Karin ran to him and threw her arms around his neck. She beamed back at Professor.

"He laughed! He laughed! Did you see, Professor, did you hear?"

She squeezed her donkey tight.

"Oh, Bellissimo," she cried, "you haven't forgotten how to laugh after all!"

Chapter 11

THE ROAD was a ribbon unwinding, glittering in the heat. The boy's shoes that were too large for Karin scraped and skidded in the gravel. It grew harder and harder to lift them. How much longer could it be to St. Raphael's Hospital?

Karin watched Professor's legs falter a little, his heels hesitate and drag. Was she imagining it or was he walking now with a slight stoop? She began to listen intently to his breathing. She compared his breathing to her own. She breathed deeper, matching hers to his. He smiled when he caught her glance but she knew he was very tired. They ought to stop to rest. Professor ought to have an hour's sleep in the shade. How wrong it was of her to allow him to make this journey down the length of Germany, all for her, all to save Bellissimo!

They climbed still another hill. The steps of Brother Christopher, too, followed one another more and more slowly. Bellissimo's head drooped low. The dust from their walking drove into his nostrils.

"Professor, please—" Karin ventured. "You must ride on Bellissimo for a while. You can fit your legs in front of Brother Christopher's chocolate bags."

Professor refused. He wagged a finger at her.

"If anyone rides, it must be you! I'm the knight, you're the princess, remember!"

She raised her arms in a helpless gesture to Brother Christopher. She wished she could tell him about her fears for Professor, about the anxiety that had not left her since Fräulein Krone had said he would collapse in the road, about his stumbling in Aachen, about how happy she would be when it was time to rest—for Professor's sake.

But at the brow of the next hill Brother Christopher gave a shout.

"There it is! We'll get there in time for the celebration all right! I began to think we might be late. See, there's the spire of their little chapel. We can almost say we're there!"

Still it seemed enough walking for a whole day before they reached the wide center door of St. Raphael's Hospital.

"You have arrived, Brother Christopher! You have arrived in time after all! Welcome to your friends, two-footed and four-footed! I'm Sister Catherine." A young woman in a black habit threw the door open wide.

Karin curtsied and smiled into a kindly oval face framed by a stiff white wimple.

"And what are you called, child?" The wimple, Karin noticed, dug into the woman's cheeks and made them bulge.

"Karin Steiner, Miss, I mean—" She did not know how to address a nun.

"Well, Karin, you must be a fairy in our parade. We have an extra costume and you're just the right size for it. And you, my dear sir—" Sister Catherine turned to Professor.

"With a lovely mustache like yours, you must be our wizard! What a pity we can't turn you into a clown, Brother Christopher. You'd make a superb clown, but we need you as you are to add dignity to the occasion. As for the donkey—" Sister Catherine swept past to hold Bellissimo's head in her hands. "We'll decorate him with crepe-paper flowers and he can pull the little cart full of gifts! How the children will shout when they see him!"

A group of older girls in brown smocks hurried to make Bellissimo comfortable. They unstrapped his saddlebags, led him to the grassy plot at one side of the courtyard and brought him a bucket of water. Bellissimo took a long lingering drink, almost forgetting he hated water.

A second nun had been watching from the doorway. She was tall and broad, with stern bright eyes. Sister Catherine ran to her, laughing, brimming with her new ideas for the parade. She called to the guests:

"Come and meet Sister Agnes. She's worked harder for the celebration than anyone else!"

"But I cannot agree about the donkey!" said Sister Agnes abruptly. "It's an impossible idea. What would Mother Beatrice say?"

Karin and Professor stared at each other. This was Sister Agnes! This was the aunt who was to help them, this woman who disapproved of Bellissimo!

They followed her meekly indoors, Sister Catherine in their midst, along the corridor to a big room where the costumes were being finished. Three nuns were decorating the gift cart with crepe-paper flowers and streamers. Older girls in brown smocks were shirring crepe-paper ruffles for the row of younger girls under the window.

Sister Agnes stood in the middle of the room giving instructions. Her first words to Karin were "Go and wash, child. Go straight through to the end of the corridor."

But the argument about Bellissimo began again and Karin lingered, tiptoeing here and there so Sister Agnes would not notice her.

What a shrill voice she had! And how indignant she was, battling against the whole room, one against the fifteen or twenty women and girls who wanted Bellissimo in the parade.

"I consider it a preposterous idea! Mother Beatrice will return shortly. And what is to greet her in the corridor? A donkey! It would bite someone or kick! And I'm sure it wouldn't be—sanitary. It most likely has fleas!"

"Oh, no, Sister," Karin blurted out from a corner of the room. "Bellissimo is very clean, only a bit dusty from the journey. And he dearly loves children. He wouldn't think of biting or kicking them!"

"And we'll wash him!" volunteered one of the girls in brown. "We'll scrub him all over!"

"And his hoofs, his hoofs!" cried Sister Agnes above the rising din. "They'll clop, clop, clop and give the poorly children headache!"

The girls thought of a cure for that, too. Three of them set to work making bootees for Bellissimo out of lint.

Sister Agnes was on the point of saying the great flat "No!" which would have meant there was no hope of

Bellissimo's walking in the parade. Her lips had formed a tight line. Her face had turned a brilliant pink. All around the room women and girls held their breaths—the girls fastening together the flowers for Bellissimo's head, the girls holding the lint, Sister Catherine, puzzling how to attach Bellissimo to the cart—

Professor drew from his pocket the letter from Frau Maggold and handed it to Sister Agnes with a bow.

Then a small gentle old nun entered the room. Sister Agnes did not say her no after all. Her face became still. The old lady helped Karin tie the last flowers to her crown, draw on her crepe-paper costume and attach her wings. Bellissimo was led in, sleek and proud and energetic.

"The children will be enchanted with your donkey!" the old lady said softly. "You must dress him yourself, so he won't feel strange. As I was coming across the courtyard I found some of the girls about to give him a bath, poor little donkey! I made them brush the dust away instead. If there's one thing a donkey hates, it's baths!"

Karin glanced at Sister Agnes and found her nodding in agreement.

"I know!" said Karin. She and the old lady fitted the flower chain over Bellissimo's ears and knelt to tie on his lint socks. It was not difficult to harness him to the cart because the girth, which Sister Catherine brought from the hospital barn, exactly fitted him. Soon he was ready, splendid and vain between the shafts of the wagon. His eyes shone and twinkled as they had when he had played tag with the boys in the meadow.

A big girl hovered about till she could catch the old nun's attention.

"Is it time, Mother Beatrice?" she asked. "Shall I go tell them to ring the bells?"

"It is time, child. Just give me a chance to run round to the other end of the ward, where I can watch the children's

faces," said Mother Beatrice. Before she hurried away, she took Karin's hand.

"I'm delighted you and your dear old friend and your donkey have come to celebrate with us!"

The bells of the little chapel next to the hospital rang out to announce the party. All the children in the hospital's four wards had been crowded into one huge ell-shaped ward. The beds were placed close together in two long rows. As

the doors opened for the parade to begin, there was an excited
chorus of shouts, followed by a deep hush. The band went
first, a company of girls in brown with flower crowns and
crepe-paper sashes. On flutes, shepherd pipes, cymbals and
triangles they played a rollicking tune. Next came a cluster
of ballerinas, dancing and bowing; next three girls in fairy
costumes like Karin's, holding a long flower chain.

And then, drawing his cart trimmed with streamers and
flowers, came Bellissimo, with Karin to guide him.

There was a long "Ohhhhhh!" of surprise. There were
cries and giggles and squeals of joy.

"A donkey! It's a real live donkey!"

"Oh, isn't he wonderful!"

"He's so small and lovely!"

"Look at his boots. Look at the flowers on him! Oh, I wish
I could touch him!"

The only trouble was that Bellissimo wouldn't stay in
line. At first he walked correctly, with measured step, but
all at once he gave a loud "Eeea!" and began to prance.
Then he backed, upsetting the wizard's starry hat, setting
Brother Christopher's cluster of balloons sailing around the
ward. He romped and gamboled and skidded, ears and tail
flying. He was remembering Brother Christopher's road-
teaser and trying to do it again.

How the children laughed!

Karin grasped Bellissimo's mane with both hands. Even
then he hopped and sprang about, tossing the petals from
his flower garland. The more the children laughed and
shouted, the gayer he became.

Karin took hold of his head and scolded him, scowling

straight into his eyes. He tried to wriggle away, but she held tight, and now only his ears and his tail waved to the music. Karin walked backward, holding her donkey's head firmly, all the way to the end of the ward. For a while after the parade finished and the music stopped, she held on, laughing in spite of herself because Bellissimo's gaze was woeful and crestfallen, because his flower chain had come loose from one ear and now drooped over his forehead.

There was an apple and a toy for everyone. The girls were given dolls made by the nuns and the helpers. The boys had wooden trucks made by the hospital janitor. Next came Brother Christopher's balloons, captured again, and his chocolate bars from Philadelphia. Some of the children who had been tiny when the war began had never tasted chocolate before. There were little cakes decorated with sugar flowers, and pink puddings, each with a blob of cream on top. The children blinked, dazzled by the parade, by the balloons and flowers, by Bellissimo, by the good things on their trays.

When all the gifts and food had been shared out, and a trayful had been brought to Karin, and an apple to Bellissimo, Mother Beatrice stepped to the center of the ward and everyone bowed his head. Mother Beatrice prayed:

"Come, Lord Jesus, be our guest,
And bless this feast Thou gavest us. Amen."

At once the clatter of spoons began. The nuns, the helpers and Brother Christopher darted here and there, helping the younger ones. Mother Beatrice and Professor stood side-by-side in the center of the ward, their chins lifted, their eyes soft and dreamy. The noisier the children became, the more genially they smiled. With their merry faces and their twin robes they looked like brother and sister. "But of course," Karin chuckled to Bellissimo, "they aren't really a bit alike. How surprised Mother Beatrice would be if she knew that Professor is very likely a sort of magician!"

Only one of the patients was not eating. In the bed at the corner of the ell a blonde girl strained forward to watch Karin seat herself at the little table at the far end of the ward. The girl stared intently at Karin's face, she watched each bite Karin took, each movement of her hands.

When Sister Catherine went to the girl to ask her why she did not eat, she whispered tremblingly, "That girl— please, Sister, I know her. She's Karin!"

Sister Catherine smoothed the girl's sheets, tucked her in firmly, and kissed her forehead. She crossed the ward and touched Karin's shoulder.

"We have someone here who knows you. I would have thought she was imagining it but she seems to know your name."

Karin turned, followed Sister Catherine's pointing finger, and recognized Marianne.

At first Karin could not move. It was as if someone had thrown a bucketful of freezing water over her. Shiver after shiver ran through her. She wanted to fly to Marianne's bed but she could not even get up from her chair. Then, pale and trembling, she held Sister Catherine's hand as she walked down the aisle. When she reached Marianne's bedside she stood staring, managing no more than a whisper.

"I—I've been looking for you all along the way! Why didn't you shout to me? I didn't even see you!"

But then Marianne smiled her old gleeful mischievous smile, and Karin threw her arms around her and hugged her with all her might. Soon both girls were laughing loudly and Marianne was calling Bellissimo with the piercing whistle she had used for him in Julich days. It wasn't until Brother Christopher arrived at the foot of the bed with Karin's trayful of food that the girls drew away from each other and blushed deeply, aware of the dozens of pairs of eyes trained upon them.

"Two old friends have found each other again!" exclaimed Brother Christopher. "That's a wonderful ending to our parade! But don't forget to eat, you two!"

Karin and Marianne stayed together, matching spoonfuls of pudding, stopping to grin at each other.

"Finding you—well, it's the nicest thing that's happened since—" Karin did not finish her sentence. A shadow settled over her happiness and Marianne's. After a silence Karin asked, "How long have you been here?"

"It's a funny thing. I don't know," said Marianne.

"A long, long time? Since—that day? Oh, but you weren't in Julich that day."

"I don't remember everything that happened before I came here," said Marianne. "There are gaps—but I remembered you the minute I saw you! Oh, Karin, I remembered you! And dear old Bellissimo, I remembered him! Just look at him now!"

Bellissimo had backed the wagon and turned it this way and that but he could not wedge himself between the beds to get to Karin. He had to be contented to wait at the foot of Marianne's bed, nuzzling the bedclothes and making his grating noise at the back of his throat. Soon the helpers came to lead him around for all the children to see.

"Remember the meadow where we used to canter?" "Remember the yellow butterfly? We laid it down and thought it was dead, and then it flew away!"

"I remember," said Karin. "Remember our school, and Fräulein Dolmer, and the stream and—" She thought of her sister Gerti, of how she and Marianne used to make a chair with their hands to carry the little girl across the stream.

"Why do they keep you here?" she asked. "Are you ill?"

"My leg," said Marianne.

Karin looked down at the bedclothes.

"I lost my leg," said Marianne quickly. "But only below the knee. They're going to give me an artificial one. I'll be able to walk again." Marianne lifted her eyes to Sister Agnes, watching from the foot of the bed. She caught Sister Agnes' eye and raised her chin and smiled. It seemed to Karin that Marianne had been taught by the Sisters to smile like that.

Sister Agnes put her finger against her lips to tell Karin and Marianne to be quiet while Brother Christopher gave his little talk. The talk was about the anniversary and about a peaceful world. All through it, Karin's eyes kept stealing back to Marianne, to her thin cheeks and hollow eyes, to the colorless strands of hair that had been blonde and curly and bright before—

Karin was allowed to stay with Marianne after the party

was over, during the hour when the boys and girls were being wheeled back to their own wards. They talked together in hushed tones, half afraid to speak of the past. And though they kept to the littlest memories, their sorrows piled up and up, and they were helpless to stop the mountain growing.

"Sometimes I wake in the morning," whispered Marianne, "and hide my head in my pillow and cry—softly so they won't hear. I—I don't want to stay here, on and on. I wake up in the night and it feels so lonely. I don't seem to belong anywhere. Oh, Karin, isn't it terrible that we can't have our homes again ever!"

"I, too," whispered Karin. "I think about Mother and Daddy and Gerti all the time—"

"I wish we could stay together," whispered Marianne. "Then at least we'd have somebody."

Karin began to tidy Marianne's hair. She smoothed it back, running her fingers through it.

"Tell me where you're going," said Marianne. "The Sisters told us there would be an old man and a little girl in the parade, stopping here for a while on their way to Switzerland."

What was there to tell Marianne that wouldn't make her feel even lonelier than before? Should she say that the Children's Village was for children who had lost everyone in the war?

Not only had Marianne lost her parents, she had been hurt. She would never be able to run across a meadow again.

If she told Marianne the words of Professor's, which she had gone over so many times that she knew them perfectly by heart: "It's full of children from many nations, all living happily together. There's no hunger and no loneliness—"

No one needed to belong to the Village more than Marianne. Marianne had no Bellissimo. She had no one at all.

Marianne was watching Karin's face, wondering why she kept silent.

"I think—" Karin began hesitantly. "I don't know very much about it. It's a little cluster of houses for children to live in. I don't know—" She wanted to make it seem unimportant.

"What don't you know?"

Karin steered the subject away. "Did you notice anything strange about Professor?"

"The old man? I noticed he was a wizard."

"I don't mean that. Did you look at his face?"

"He has a lovely laughing face and a white mustache."

"Yes, but his eyes—"

"Is there something strange about him?"

"I don't know. I don't understand him. Do you know, sometimes I think he must be—magic," whispered Karin. "So many wonderful things have happened. It began right away, the first day. There was the roped-together family. Then there was Frau Lang. She went with us and found her daughter and her granddaughter. And the boy, there was the boy— We took him to the hospital and he was all right. And Eric got a new pair of trousers and I these shoes —and then we came here and I found you!" Karin glanced at the ceiling.

"It's been like—like a lot of miracles all along the way!

I wonder, Marianne, do you think God might have picked out Professor to use as a sort of guardian angel? Even if he's only a man, I mean, not a real angel? Have you ever heard of God turning somebody into an angel without having him die first?"

Perplexity reflected back from Marianne's eyes.

"I've never heard of anybody like that, an angel and a man at the same time. Does he say his prayers?"

"Sometimes he looks up at the sky and sort of mumbles, but it's in English and I can't understand."

"Maybe he really is a wizard!" whispered Marianne.

"He doesn't look like a wizard," said Karin. "He looks more like a guardian angel, the way I'd imagine a guardian angel to look, except that he has no wings. But there's the prism. It makes everything sparkle, and he always seems to have it in his hand when the wonderful things happen. So how could it be God he speaks to? God wouldn't have anything to do with a magic prism! He must be a wizard or an elf or a goblin of some kind. But if he is, and can make things happen by magic, why is he so worried about getting Bellissimo across the border, and about arriving at the Children's Village on time?"

Karin and Marianne each gave a little shiver and a hunch of shoulders. Their heads jerked round simultaneously when they heard a rustling at the end of the bed.

It was Sister Catherine.

"I've come for you, Karin," she said.

"Bellissimo—" Karin realized that she had not seen her donkey for half an hour at least.

"He's one reason I've come," said Sister Catherine. "We've

put him in the barn. We've made him as comfortable as we know how, but he's out there braying most mournfully. We can only think he must be missing you."

"I'll go to him. He's used to my saying good night to him, you see. He'll be all right when I talk to him a bit." Karin reached out to Marianne.

"In any case it's past Marianne's bedtime—and yours." Sister Catherine took Karin's hand to draw her away.

But Marianne held tight to Karin's other hand.

"You didn't say how long you're staying. Stay a few days at least!"

Karin shook her head. All she could promise was, "I won't go away without seeing you, Marianne. Good night!"

She kissed Marianne and followed Sister Catherine out of the ward, along a corridor and out across a brick quadrangle to the barn which rang with Bellissimo's brays.

It was only necessary to hug Bellissimo and assure him that she would be near, that she would see him again in the morning. How still the outdoors seemed when she left the barn again! Now that there was no more braying, she could hear the squeak of her shoes against the bricks, and the rustle of Sister Catherine's habit.

They hurried along another corridor to the reception room where Professor and Brother Christopher sat talking and drinking hot chocolate. On the table was a mugful of chocolate for Karin, too.

"I'll come back for her in ten minutes," said Sister Catherine. With a thoughtful, quizzical expression she added, "I did not know that a donkey is capable of a positively dog-like devotion. And I've never admired a donkey as much as

I do tonight. Bellissimo is a gentleman. He didn't forget his manners once during the celebration." Sister Catherine took a step nearer and smiled straight at Professor. "And what has come over Sister Agnes? Have you put a magic spell on her? I found her in the library reading about donkeys. I must run now and see what she's thought of next. It's all most astonishing!"

Lamplight fell on Karin as she drank her chocolate. Professor went on talking about America to Brother Christopher, but every little while his glance strayed to Karin. Finally he said gently, "You're troubled about your friend back there in the ward—"

Karin moved to the stool at Professor's feet. She bent forward, her finger tracing a pattern on the carpet. She swallowed again and again and could not look up. Not a minute before, as she was sipping the chocolate, an idea had struck her like a flash bulb exploding. It had made her heart leap, it had made her gulp and nearly choke. Now it seemed that to tell Professor about it would be harder than walking the fourteen miles to St. Raphael's Hospital.

She took a very deep breath and began to speak, though she hadn't enough courage left to look into Professor's face.

"I was wishing—I just suddenly began to wish—that Marianne could join us over there in Switzerland—not now but when she has her new leg and can walk and—by the end of the summer maybe, if—if there would be room for her."

She waited. Her heart beat wildly. She felt suffocated, as if a stone were stuck in her throat.

"She has no family, no aunt or uncle even, no grandparents?" asked Professor after a pause.

"I don't know about her aunt. She had only one aunt, I remember. She hadn't any sisters or brothers. She lost her mother and father in Julich—that same day."

An eternity seemed to go by before Professor raised himself from his chair and left the room. Karin sat in a crumpled heap on the stool. Brother Christopher studied her and said nothing.

It was such a simple idea, having Marianne at the Village. Karin wondered she had not thought of it right away, the moment she saw her friend again. It was such a wonderful idea! There must surely be something wrong with it, something to make it impossible, some reason why she should never have mentioned it at all. It would be terrible if it turned out to be impossible! It would be so marvelous if it worked out! Oh, it was dangerous, it was expecting too much of the magic, dreaming as she was of the future with Marianne at her side!

Professor returned so softly that neither Karin nor Brother Christopher heard him until he was within the ring of lamplight and touched Karin's head.

She started and looked up. He held the prism in his fingers, but she knew it was more than the prism that was making a new life for Marianne. It was wonderful, magical old Professor himself!

With a cry of joy Karin jumped up, threw out her arms and hugged him, her face pressed so tight against his waistcoat that she came away with two red button marks on her right cheek.

Chapter 12

THEY GATHERED to leave St. Raphael's Hospital early the next morning. Brother Christopher decided to walk with them a little way to enjoy their company. A nine-year-old boy named Birdy was to ride on Bellissimo. Birdy had come to the hospital with a crushed kneecap. Now he was better, but not able to walk very far. He lived twelve miles to the south, and when he got home, he said, he would ask his father to drive Karin, Professor and Bellissimo a distance toward the border. His father had a truck which needed no gas and would run on anything that burned. It was very smoky; you had to face the other way if you sat in back. But at least it went!

Birdy was thrilled that he would be home by late afternoon, and above all that he was to ride home on a donkey. He sat on Bellissimo as if glued there.

"Why does your donkey keep waggling his ears?" he asked Karin.

"Oh, that's his way of talking," said Karin.

"Well then, Bellissimo," said Birdy, "will you let me ride you right up to the gate so my mother and father and brother can see me?"

Bellissimo's ears promised: "I'll do better than that. I'll carry you through the front door!"

Karin stretched up her arms and laughed. How fresh and clean she felt with her hair newly washed and brushed, the crepe-paper crown of flowers round it, and all her clothes washed and ironed once again! How fine Bellissimo looked this morning in his newly laundered saddlebags! And how eager he was to be off!

"Come on! What are we waiting for?" shouted his ears.

A nun brought Marianne in a wheel chair to say good-by. She had changed back to the Marianne that Karin remembered, her merry friend who tossed her head and laughed often and could not stop talking, not merely talking but exclaiming in happiness. Karin stayed close to her while a parting speech was made by Professor, who stood near Bellissimo and had to shield his mustache with his hat. There was a prayer from Mother Beatrice: "that they may overcome all their troubles and journey on with courage and trust in Thee." Karin bent over Marianne, grasping both her arms. There was no more time, but Marianne held her with a burst of talking:

"I'm going to start practicing at the bars today, learning to walk again. Oh, Karin, when I woke up this morning and they told me about coming to be with you, it was"— she gulped—"it was like just being born! All the rest was a dream and now it's real, now I've come alive!" She dropped her voice to a whisper. "It doesn't matter what sort of place it is, it doesn't matter if it's magic or anything, as long as you'll be there, too!"

One smile, so huge and radiant it was like a single smile, spread from Karin and Marianne to all the group gathered in the doorway.

The chapel bells began to ring, as they had for the party. Bellissimo's ears jerked up. He gave a mirthful bray and struck out for Switzerland, with Birdy hooting gleefully on his back. Brother Christopher and Professor rushed after him to grab his saddlebags. He carried them along with him. They could only wave their free arms and shout.

All at once Bellissimo thought of Karin. He came to a skidding stop and twisted his head round. A second bray welled up inside him, the pathetic bray he used to call Karin.

She sprinted down the drive to him. By then the little procession was halfway to the gates; it was too late for anything more than waves and shouts.

"Good-by, everyone! Thank you for the hospitality! God bless you! Good-by!"

The nuns and Marianne kept waving until the hospital wall hid the travelers from sight. And after that they stood quietly looking down the drive, past the shrubbery, through the trees, toward the last point where it had been possible to see their guests. Marianne kept on smiling, and at the same time her chin was trembling and her eyes brimming with tears. She held her right hand against her cheek to stop the breeze's taking Karin's kiss away.

It was jolly to be striding out in the morning sun with Brother Christopher and the merry mischievous Birdy. Soon, pointing jauntily at here a tree, there a rock, Birdy showed how he had earned his nickname. Not only could he whistle so you would think a dozen birds were swooping about your head, but he could make the whistling thinner and thinner, so you thought the birds were flying away, and then, to witt! he'd bring them back again. The most remarkable thing about Birdy's whistling was that it seemed to come from everywhere but from him. There was nothing about his face to show he was the whistler. Not even his lips moved. But his eyes twinkled and shone.

Another surprising thing happened: Brother Christopher began to sing Wagner in his big bass voice, turning the countryside for a mile around into a concert hall. Professor laughed in delight.

"Before you became Brother Christopher," he said, "your name wasn't Peter Gunther by any chance, was it?"

"It was," said Brother Christopher.

"In that case," Professor laughed, "I've been to New York especially to hear you, and I have five or six records of your voice at home, and we are strolling along through Germany with a famous man!"

A mile from the hospital, at the place where the road bent uphill, Brother Christopher said good-by. He gave Karin the notes he and Mother Beatrice had written in hopes of helping Bellissimo across the border. He announced:

"We haven't said anything to Marianne yet, Karin, but I shall be the one to bring her to join you at the Children's Village. I'm going along today to the American Army camp near here to see if I can borrow a jeep and a driver for a day to carry us as far as the border. So it isn't good-by after all, it's just so long! I'll be seeing you! When Marianne and

I get there, we'll have a grand concert! Take care of them all, Bellissimo!"

Brother Christopher turned back toward the hospital, walking his easy bouncy walk and stopping now and then to wave. Distance dwarfed him till he looked a lone penguin under the wide blue sky, stopping to raise a wing and hurrying on to turn into a black mouse, a beetle, a gnat, nothing—

Karin smiled across at Professor, up at Birdy. How like a happy dream everything was!

"It's a lovely day," she said. "What do you like best, Birdy?"

"Out of everything there is?" asked Birdy.

"Yes."

"Oh, my mother and my father and my brother, though he's a pest sometimes—and this donkey," said Birdy. "I guess Bellissimo is a very valuable donkey, isn't he?"

"Yes, he is. I wouldn't sell him for a million marks."

"And what do you like best, Karin?" The question came from Professor.

Karin thought earnestly before she answered.

"I'm very fond of Bellissimo. I'm so fond of him that if anybody's unkind to him I don't like that person at all. I love him better than anybody—anybody alive. I mean—" She finished in an awed hushed voice. "Except you." She blushed and gazed out over the mountains. "But I like lots of things, especially animals. And I like anything to do with fairies and elves and gnomes and goblins and things— and magic." She stole a look across at the prism. "I heard once," she went on, "that if you say you don't believe in fairies, a fairy will die. Do you think that's true, Professor?"

"I shouldn't be a bit surprised."

"And would the same be true of elves and goblins and sprites and things?"

"Why not?"

"And do you yourself believe in fairies and things?"

"'Course not!" Birdy butted in.

"Oh, Birdy," wailed Karin, "one might have died just then! You believe in them, don't you, Professor?"

"Oh my, yes. Why do you ask?"

"I just wondered. An elf, now. Would he necessarily have wings like a fairy?"

"Elves don't have wings," said Professor.

"But they can fly," Karin said uncertainly.

"Of course they can. They simply lift their arms and soar through the air like Peter Pan and Wendy. You've heard of Peter Pan and Wendy?"

Karin hadn't. She gulped.

"But I suppose if an animal were to fly," she said, "he'd need wings?"

"I should think if it were Bellissimo, his ears would be enough!" Professor laughed. "What a question box you are this morning!"

Again Karin sighed. She had come all this way, she was drawing nearer and nearer to Switzerland, and she was no nearer to understanding who and what Professor was!

They passed through a village quite untouched by the war, with a fountain at its center. They found a forgotten hamlet where grass grew between the cobbles and there was only one old couple to be seen. They found villages sleeping over their war hurts, but they came upon no village so badly shattered as Julich. Soon there were no more villages at all. The mountains rose higher, the forests grew taller, and gray-brown rocks lay about as if rolled down from the mountaintops. A cooling breeze sprang up, rustling and soughing the trees in a music that was happy and sad both at once.

The road ran uphill and they lost sight of the river. The air grew still cooler and a heavier breeze came up behind them, as if to hurry them on their way. Time was growing terribly short. They had only two days left to reach the Village. Birdy's father must help them if there was to be any chance at all of arriving on time. Before them a flock of swallows sped across the sky as if they, too, were anxious and hurrying.

They entered a landscape of gorges and defiles. Clouds began to gather, hustling over the hills. One great dark cloud which was like a wall slid up behind them. The sun grew hazy. It became hard to tell exactly where it was in the sky.

They curved around a wild overgrown mountain, all rock and forest, lonely and silent except for bleating from an occasional flock of sheep. Karin could tell that Professor was searching for shelter, for a shepherd's hut perhaps or a shed. The sky grew darker, till only the dandelions along the roadsides showed, thousands of gold watches with blurred faces.

The black wall caught up; it began to close over them. The branches of the trees and bushes sawed at one another. The wind tried to tear the bags loose from Bellissimo's sides. Still there was no rain, but the fields, the mountains, the road went black as night.

It was Professor who brought Bellissimo to a stop by giving his tail a tug.

"We'll borrow one of Bellissimo's rugs for you, Karin. Birdy must wear my raincoat. We'll shelter against those rocks across the field. It's just a thundershower. It will pass. There'll be sun again soon."

Birdy was helped down to the road. Buckles were loosened and one of the rugs was tugged from Bellissimo's back. Karin took off her crepe-paper crown and packed it into one of the bags. Professor brought out his plastic raincoat and sou'wester, folded inside a plastic envelope.

"You wear it, Professor," coaxed Karin. "We enjoy getting wet, don't we, Birdy?"

"I'll say we do!" said Birdy. "I've walked in the rain lots of times. It toughens you up, it hardens your skin!"

Protesting, Birdy felt his arms being thrust into the raincoat sleeves, felt the sou'wester being tied firmly under his chin. As he was helped back onto Bellissimo, a few large splashy drops of rain splattered into the bags.

They turned off the road and plodded across a field, along the edge of a ravine. Suddenly wind and rain, thunder and lightning struck in rapid succession, as if they had been pushing side-by-side and had finally burst through the black wall. The rain came in hard sheets, slapping their faces. Bellissimo held his head very low. Grasses thrashed his forehead. Drops flew from his shaggy coat. The rain sent its hiss echoing round the mountain, down into the ravine. The hiss grew and grew till it seemed to come from everywhere, even from under the ground.

Stunted trees marked the edge of the ravine. The wind and rain seemed to be trying to hurl them down to destruction, seemed to be trying to turn the ravine into another Rhine. They only laughed because they were together.

The storm did not pass so they went on any way. It had grown late and they were tired. Karin was worried because Professor was so wet. She was watching him and not her feet. Karin fell, twisting her ankle. The pain of it sent her whirling into darkness. When she woke Birdy was bending over her, saying, "Professor has gone for help. He'll be back." Birdy gave a little whistle to cheer her.

Karin noticed the crest of the valley-side opposite. Its trees were like church spires, their pinnacles lit up softly as if by thousands of candles. It was not candles, it was moonlight, thrusting bright fingers down into the darkness of the chasm. How long had she lain there?

Professor came and a man leading a great horse. They lifted her up—

Chapter 13

WHEN KARIN woke again it was bright morning. She heard the bubbling of water boiling, the clatter of dishes and cutlery. Professor was making breakfast.

"You've slept fifteen hours, young lady!" he called to her. "How do you feel?"

"Fine, thank you." Karin sat up, flexing her stiff hands, straightening her aching arms, wincing when her foot moved.

The man who had come with his horse called good morning in a voice like a cannon going off. In a shaft of sunlight he sat rubbing a strap with saddle soap. He dipped into a tin with his cloth and picked up a second strap. Karin noticed its sheepskin lining.

"You're cleaning Bellissimo's straps."

"Right, lass. And I've groomed him for you. He was covered with mud, that donkey of yours, and his tail tuft was full of burrs. He brayed the roof off when we put him in the barn, and had all my stock thinking the end of the world was near, but he was all right the minute we brought him to the window where he could look in and see you.

He's been there all night like a big watchdog. He hasn't taken his eyes off you!"

"Where is he?" Twisting on the coach, Karin found Bellissimo's head, framed in a side window. He blew through his nose and gave a husky bray when she called to him.

Professor introduced Karin to Herr Rulff, the farmer who had gone out into the storm to carry her to his house. Karin was surprised to see he was an old man, perhaps as old as Professor. His back was crooked and he had a long gray beard. But how huge he was! What a long way his hand had to travel to come up from his side to scratch his shaggy head! He was dressed almost entirely in leather: leather trousers to the knee, leather boots, leather waistcoat and sleeveless leather jacket—all dark and stained as if he had worn them for tens of years. And what an untidy house he lived in! Karin looked around at the long low room which had begun as a kitchen but was now living room, dining room, kitchen and storeroom combined. The windowsills were crowded with geraniums beginning to bud. One round table held a dozen old lamps, another an assortment of tools piled high. It would have taken all day to make a list of the furniture and odds and ends cluttering Herr Rulff's kitchen.

But it was a blissful kitchen, full of good breakfast smells and the drone of cheery voices. What were Professor and Birdy talking about over there by the stove—about yesterday, or about what was to be done? Questions rose in Karin's mind like bubbles from a spring, dozens of small questions and then the huge one which frightened and overwhelmed her: How can we travel farther now, when I can't walk?

Bellissimo can't carry both Birdy and me on his back. Birdy himself is almost too heavy for one small donkey.

They brought a table close to the sofa, so they could all eat together. Karin's questions began to be answered without her saying a word.

"When I left you out there I didn't know which way to turn," said Professor. "There was no house in sight in any direction. Then I ran over the brow of the hill and there was this house, the right house and the right man!"

"And that donkey of yours!" said Herr Rulff to change the subject. "Last night he had a troughful of oats, and this morning I took him a great armful of barley and hay. 'You can't eat all this,' said I. But he did!"

"Thank you very much!" Karin smiled. "But wasn't there a horse, too?"

"A huge black horse who carried Herr Rulff and me as swift as the wind to rescue you," said Professor.

Herr Rulff came to examine Karin's ankle. He held it gently in his huge hands.

"But Zurich! I'm making Professor late!" Karin blurted out. "I'm making him break his promise!"

Everyone turned to look at her.

"It's terrible about my ankle!" she cried. "We must be there by tomorrow, by three o'clock in the afternoon at the very latest!"

Herr Rulff shook his head. "And two out of three of you needing to be carried."

Professor had been waiting for a chance to speak.

"Look, Karin. I've been thanking God again and again

that you're not badly hurt. Next to that my promise to be in Zurich doesn't matter. Herr Rulff says we may stay here till your ankle is better. All that matters is that you're safe, that you'll soon be well again!"

"But I don't want you to be late! I mustn't make you late! It means so much to you to be in time for your meeting and then to catch your plane, I know it does! All this long journey—you've done it only for my sake, so I could keep Bellissimo! I mustn't make you late!" Karin hung her head. "We seemed to be—so—near!" she muttered.

Birdy edged forward.

"I'll show you how to make a whistle," he said. "I found a piece of wood—"

"It looks worse to her because she's still very tired," said Professor to Herr Rulff. "Could you help me, please, to get to the nearest place where I can send a telegram? I want to give them time to find another speaker for the meeting. As for the plane—well, when I don't appear at the airport, my friends will go on without me, that's all. I'll get in touch with them as soon as I can. They'll understand."

"But what about the reservation on the plane?" Karin persisted. "What will the men on the plane say?"

"Whatever they do say will be to an empty seat," said Professor. "Not to worry! If I were to send them a telegram, too—"

"That's right, not to worry!" interrupted Herr Rulff. "Not to worry because I have an idea!" Grinning, drawing pictures in the air with both hands, he began:

"In my barn I have an old wagon. It's only a small one

and it is clumsy. It's a hay wagon, you understand. But its wheels are sound—huge wheels they are, like water wheels. The wagon must be sixty or seventy years old. We shall line it with straw and a featherbed from upstairs—there are too many featherbeds in this house—and on top of all that, rosy and smiling, will ride the little girl!"

He flung out his arms. He threw back his head and his laugh bounced back from the ceiling and walls. "And what a racket it will make, that wagon, going down the road! There won't be a soul who misses your passing!"

He was so pleased with his idea that he shut his ears and waved aside all Professor's protests.

"But my dear Herr Rulff, how will we get the wagon back to you?"

"It doesn't matter, I don't care a jot. Look here. I've been a widower for ten years. I've lost my only son in the war. This little old wagon's no use to me."

But Birdy shouted, "We have a horse, yes, one horse. He's a very good horse, and strong, and can easily pull a hay wagon. So one day very soon, Herr Rulff, you will look out and see us coming down your lane, my father and I and our horse and the wagon, and maybe my brother will come, too!"

They were so happy and relieved they nearly forgot to eat breakfast.

Before another hour was up, the wagon was dusted and ready in the yard. Its tremendous, rusty, iron-rimmed wheels squeaked and banged and scrunched as they turned. But the featherbed on which Karin and Birdy were to ride was as soft as the bed in which the spoiled princess slept in the story of the princess and the pea.

Everything had been taken out of the saddlebags and aired in the sun. As Professor repacked, Herr Rulff added to the food supplies fresh milk and bacon and cheese. The bags were stowed at the back of the wagon, where they looked like two dumpy figures asleep with their heads lolling on their chests.

Herr Rulff roped the wagon shafts to Bellissimo's girth straps, but there was no bit in the barn small enough to fit a donkey. Professor would have to walk in front to guide Bellissimo and the wagon.

Bellissimo did not like the wagon. His ears rose like two furry exclamation marks, he shifted from one pair of legs to the other. And when Karin and Birdy were aboard and it was time to set out, he refused to move, but stood as if rooted in the mud and stones of the yard. Not even the sight of Professor's mustache a few inches before him would entice him forward.

Herr Rulff tried hauling him as he would haul a sheep to the dipping tub. Bellissimo's ears lay back now and semaphored, "Make a fool of yourself if you like. As for me, I refuse to pull a ridiculous contraption like this!"

"You're being an unreasonable animal!" lectured Professor. "We're not going off and leaving Karin! She's not ten inches behind you!" He held out the shoe Karin couldn't fit over her swollen foot.

Bellissimo's ears said, "Just what I'd expect of a bookish man! No understanding of donkeys at all!"

Karin gave a big sigh.

"He doesn't like the wagon," she said. "I'll have to try to explain things to him. I'm afraid he thinks it's beneath his dignity to pull a hay wagon."

Everybody kept silent while Karin spoke to Bellissimo.

"You're a very clever donkey, Bellissimo! I know you can pull a wagon, any sort of wagon, without even trying! Ordinary horses can pull wagons, and you're much cleverer than a horse! And it's a beautiful morning! Let's show Herr Rulff how you can trot, you clever donkey! Let's hurry on our way to Switzerland!"

As Bellissimo's hoofs began to pick their way gingerly across the yard, Karin encouraged him. "Oh, good Bellissimo! Clever, brave Bellissimo! I knew you could do it! Oh, I'm proud of you, Bellissimo!"

With hens squawking and fluttering in every direction, the wagon moved past the barn. Herr Rulff followed with long strides, squelching over the sodden ground, as far as the road they had left when the storm broke.

It would have been a happy leave-taking except for Karin's leaning out of the wagon to ask Herr Rulff, "And do you think they'll let us take Bellissimo across the border?"

"You have permits for him, haven't you?" asked Herr Rulff.

"No."

"No papers for him at all?"

Karin shook her head. Herr Rulff made a chucking sound with his tongue.

"You can't move an inch without a permit these days,"

he said. "There are more sheets of regulations than there are folk to read 'em! I spend half my days filling in forms, and I'm only a farmer, I'm not trying to go anywhere. Don't get your hopes up, Miss Karin, and you won't be too disappointed. Whatever happens, though, the donkey will want to eat. I've put a bagful of barley in the wagon there, under the straw."

They all shook hands, the three travelers thanking Herr Rulff again and again for his kindness. The wagon drew away.

"Send me a letter," he called. "I'll be wanting to know if they let the donkey through. Birdy, I'll see you in a week or two. Come for a few days if you can. Tell your parents they'll be very welcome. And your brother." He had to raise his voice more and more. "I'll show you the best fishing places!"

How lonely he must be, Karin thought, with his wife and son gone.

"He showed me his fishing tackle. I like fishing and I like old Herr Rulff," Birdy said. "I'm going to ask my dad if we can come and see him sometimes, my brother and I. Maybe we can come help him now and then, harvest times and such like."

Herr Rulff stood in the road, shading his eyes with one hand, waving with the other. He was the only person to be seen in the whole landscape, his house the only house. But maybe he won't have to be so lonely any more, thought Karin, and she gave Birdy a special smile.

Chapter 14

It was cosy in the wagon. The sun warmed the straw, the featherbed softened the jolting, the wagon's sides made good back rests. Birdy puffed out his cheeks and set to whistling. The breezes shooed the morning mist from the mountains, to make a sparkling highway for the travelers.

Professor called, "Ho! There it is—Switzerland!" And out came another poem:

> "Oh, joy, hurrah! We're off again!
> Off again? To where?
> Over the hills to Switzerland,
> Stop us if you dare!"

Only Karin couldn't smile. Bent over her flower crown, smoothing every petal between her thumb and first finger, she felt excitement mounting in her as steadily as the sun mounted the sky. If Birdy's father could help them, this would be the day when they would try to get Bellissimo across the border.

Karin dug her teeth into her lip.

"But I don't want to get there!" she whispered. "I don't want to cross over into Switzerland, not even if they let

Bellissimo stay with us! I don't want the journey to come to an end, I want it to go on and on forever—

"Because when we get there—" She stared at Professor's back, bobbing up and down as he strolled along at Bellissimo's side. "Because when we get there, you'll go away!"

As if in need of willows and rushes and glossy waves, the

road found its way back to the river again. Here and there the water was still hidden in mist, but the breezes blew at it as if it were a hot liquid needing cooling; and slowly the mist melted away.

It was Birdy who first remarked about the boat. Karin had been noticing it for some time, out in the pearly light of the Rhine. It was a low-curved boat with two men in it, rowing toward Switzerland. The current pulled against the oars and it seemed to stand still, yet it was keeping abreast.

They had grown used to stares on the journey. All along the way, people had watched them curiously as they passed, and children had shouted, "Look, a donkey!" and skipped after them a distance. This time, it seemed to Karin, they were being stared at with more than curiosity and they were being followed. Sometimes she could hardly see the boat in the glitter of sunlight. Sometimes a hill or a clump of trees hid it and she would glance ahead to the next level place, sure that she would see the boat again when they reached there.

But the river roughened and deepened and slowly the swish of oars drew to the rear. Karin could still see the boat, the men toiling at their rowing. They had no collars and their sleeves were rolled up. They were rowing faster, trying, Karin decided, to catch up.

The road and the river swerved to the right and the men were out of sight. Karin added them to her worries about Bellissimo and the future. She was certain she would see them again before long.

For their lunchtime picnic, Professor chose the shade of a giant horse chestnut tree a little distance inside a birch wood. Karin and Birdy let themselves down to the ground and helped to unfasten the wagon from Bellissimo. As they worked, the sun poked through the chestnut leaves so they could see may flies dancing up and down. They would stop dancing, all together, and suddenly begin again. Professor moved the picnic things deeper under the canopy of the oak.

Bellissimo was so thirsty that he didn't stop to munch the oats from Herr Rulff but went at once to the river. From where she perched herself with her sore ankle stiffly out in front of her, Karin could watch her donkey make a path through the bracken and reeds and lower his head to drink. There was still no sign of the boat. Could she have been wrong thinking the men were following the wagon?

It was wonderfully still. The wood swept in a shimmering ruff round the oak. Whisperings came from all sides, the tiniest, faintest sounds after the bang and clatter of the wagon wheels. It was hard to tell which sounds were the treetops rustling and which the river humming.

Birdy leaned against the oak, too sleepy to whistle. Professor sat on a grassy bank, cutting bread for Karin to butter. Why did he gaze upward every little while and bend his head to one side, then the other? Was he thinking about the plane, about his promise to his friend? Was he worried —as Karin was—about getting Bellissimo across the border? Or was he having a silent conversation with someone?

Karin's gaze followed Professor's upward. The oak was nearly motionless. Yet when she peered through the leaves, dozens of quick shining things darted about. She stared harder and they were gone—or were they hiding behind the leaves and branches?

Karin shook her head over her thoughts, and peered down the path Bellissimo had made to the river. Where was he? Had he moved behind that clump of pollard willow or through the birches? If his hoofs stuck in mud, or tangled themselves in the reeds— If the men in the boat stole up and clamped his jaws tight so he couldn't bray—

It was on the tip of her tongue: "I'll just run and see if Bellissimo's all right," when she remembered she couldn't walk. She would have to sit there where she was and call him. She would have to call him loudly, but she didn't want Professor and Birdy to know she was anxious. If only Bellissimo would come back where she could see him. If she could see even a tip of one ear—

Her heart gave a bump. There, beyond the end of the path, out in the river, was the boat. The men were backing water, turning, coming in stern first. They were nearing the shore. They must be very close to Bellissimo.

Karin gave a tremendous shout, "Bellissimo!"

Professor and Birdy jumped, jerked their heads around. They, too, saw the boat. They both stood up.

"I'll go," said Professor.

But there was no need. Along the path came Bellissimo, trotting zestfully, easing up to nudge Karin and Professor, coming to rest with his neck arched over Karin, his ears pricked to listen to the boat come in.

Karin grew calm now that Bellissimo was with them again. Why should she be afraid? Even when the men joined them—she was sure they would—they would merely ask if they could buy Bellissimo. Well, Professor would tell them there was no chance of that, Bellissimo was not for sale.

The plosh of oars changed to a champing and grinding against the bank. There was the rumble of arguing or grumbling. Ferns and willow branches hanging over the water's edge caught at the oars and trailed down the men's backs. The boat swung sideways and the men jumped out.

Professor sat quietly watching. Bellissimo moved closer to Karin and stroked her shoulder with his muzzle. Birdy began to whistle softly.

Branches snapped as the men pushed their way like swimmers battling the surf, along Bellissimo's thread of track.

They burst free of the reeds and bracken and walked into the clearing under the oak. They were tidier than they had seemed when out in the river. They had taken time before coming ashore to put on jackets and ties. The blond swarthy man in the lead carried two small cases, the short olive-skinned man behind was half-hidden under his burdens: a shovel, a length of pipe, a frying pan, and a newspaper bundle.

The burly man did the talking; in fact he talked so loudly that he filled the wood with noise.

"Ah, good afternoon! What a pleasant little gathering! So the donkey belongs to you. We noticed it at the river's edge. We're on our way to Switzerland. Are you, too? Let us introduce ourselves. My name's Hans Hellmann and this is my friend, Gottfried Selbig. We're Swiss. Are you?"

Professor and Birdy shook hands with the men. Karin couldn't stand up very quickly because of her ankle. She steadied herself against the tree and balanced on her good leg.

Professor reached out to her. "And this is Karin."

Karin gave a forced smile.

"What a charming little girl. Makes a picture with her flower crown. Queen of the May! She's your granddaughter?"

"I wish she were," said Professor.

"And the donkey— He's a friendly little chap. And you've a wagon, too. Just the thing for a nice day. Fine little wagon, most out-of-the-ordinary." (As if they hadn't been staring at it steadily during the past two hours! thought Karin.) "You'll be taking the wagon across the border?"

"The donkey, yes, we trust so, but not the wagon. We'll be leaving Birdy and the wagon after a few more miles." An idea came to Professor. "You were perhaps hoping we might carry your boat over into Switzerland on the wagon? We're very sorry—"

"Oh, no, no! We hadn't thought of any such thing. We've no idea of taking the boat across." The burly man changed the subject.

"We've caught some fish. We're going to make a fire and fry them. Have some with us!"

He took off his jacket. His shirt sleeves were rolled up almost to his shoulders. He thrashed about in the undergrowth, gathering stalks and twigs and branches. The small dark man scuttled after him.

The big man dug a hole with the shovel into the side of a mound. When he had scooped out the hole, he dug a second smaller hole straight down to it and fitted the pipe into it. Birdy came closer to watch. The kindling was stacked to a pyramid in the hole and very soon a thread of blue smoke rose through the pipe and into the branches of the chestnut tree. The men hurried into the woods for more twigs and branches. Birdy squatted close to the fire, puffing at it to get it to draw.

Soon smoke filled the birch wood. Karin's eyes smarted, but she, too, limped closer to sniff the smell of cooking fish, to look at the pan where they lay sizzling, each cut in half with its head and backbone removed.

The men wiped their fingers on the grass, sat down on the mound and lit cigarettes. There was nothing to do now but wait for the fish to cook.

Professor cut more bread and passed it to Karin for buttering. Birdy seated himself close to the fire. Karin could tell he admired the men's skill in making a fireplace with a real chimney. He whistled as he watched the smoke billow from the pipe.

Herr Hellmann began to talk again, to ask more questions. His first sentences were an admission that back in the river he had been watching Bellissimo and the wagon.

"I couldn't understand how you were making the donkey go. There didn't seem to be any reins."

"You're right, there weren't any. Karin has trained her donkey to obey without them," said Professor.

"Oh, the donkey belongs to the little girl. She's a lucky little one to own a donkey. It's a funny thing. I could have sworn you had four kids in the wagon, not two." Herr Hellmann pulled at the lobes of his ears.

"The two fat children at the back are Bellissimo's saddle-bags," said Professor. He and Herr Hellmann laughed.

"You planning to cross the border this evening?" Herr Hellmann asked.

"Yes," said Professor, "with help from the Lord and Birdy's father. I want to catch a plane tomorrow afternoon in Zurich."

The fish tasted delicious. Karin, eating hers a little apart from the others, studied the two men intently. Even when they weren't speaking or moving about she watched them. Herr Hellmann was too familiar, he asked too many questions. And why did the little dark man keep glancing at Bellissimo and the wagon? And why did the two men catch each other's attention, why did Herr Hellmann point with his thumb over his shoulder?

Professor seemed quite unaware that anything was wrong. There he sat, rosy-cheeked, nodding and smiling, enjoying the fish, passing round the buttered bread. When the picnic was over and the things put away, he bowed genially to the strangers.

"You'll walk along with us a distance?"

"Nice of you to ask," said Herr Hellmann, "but no, thank you. We've some business to see to before we cross into Switzerland. We'll give you a hand hitching up the donkey."

Another quick glance passed between the two men. Herr Selbig walked to the other side of the wagon. Karin's eyes followed his slightest movement. She saw him bend over one of the saddlebags, picking at the buckles of its straps, quickly reaching down—

A rage so fierce she could scarcely keep from crying out brought Karin to her feet. She limped and hopped stealthily around Bellissimo, her head and shoulders bent. She came up behind Herr Selbig, misjudged the distance and jolted against the wagon's side.

"What the—" Herr Selbig's arm flew up out of the saddlebag. His look over his shoulder was startled, then menacing. His black eyes narrowed.

But in an instant he was stroking his chin and grinning.

"Dropped my nail clippers straight into that bag there. Thought we'd have to empty it out to find them, but here they are."

He produced a pair of small chrome nail clippers. Had he brought them from the bag or had he taken them from his pocket? Karin glanced back at Professor, chatting with Herr Hellmann. Bellissimo came up behind and thrust his head between Karin and Herr Selbig.

The men helped hitch Bellissimo to the wagon. Again Karin grew calmer. They were leaving the picnic spot now and nothing terrible had happened. There had not even been an offer to buy Bellissimo.

"Good-by!" she called with Professor and Birdy. "See you in Switzerland!"

They rode safely away, but she could not forget Herr Selbig's eyes when she had surprised him: cold and surly and secretive and threatening. "If you dare tell," they seemed to say. Had he wanted to rob them? Did he think there was something valuable in the saddlebags, watches or jewels perhaps? Or had his nail clippers really slipped out of his pocket?

Karin sighed and turned her eyes toward the blue and purple mountains of Switzerland. There was enough to worry about, enough to wonder about, enough to hope, without puzzling over two odd strangers.

Chapter 15

THEY WENT on into the lovely afternoon. The nearer they drew to Birdy's farm, the more he whistled and bragged.

"We've got a grand big barn, and two big fields, and the biggest horse you ever saw, bigger than Herr Rulff's. And my Dad's strong, he's as strong as ten men put together, and we've got—"

"A big rhinoceros and a big hippopotomus and a big head, too!" scolded Karin, laughing.

Birdy was too happy to take offense. He made up new whistle songs, trilling higher and louder and longer with each, stopping only to give directions: "To the left now, around that curve, up that little hump— We're here! We're home! Hey there, *Mutti, Vadi,* we're home! Hurry up, we're home!" He stood up in the wagon and nearly fell overboard waving.

Karin and Professor were swept into the house and wrapped round and round with hospitality. They were urged and urged to stay. A week? Well then, overnight at least? Oh, dear, well, for a good meal anyway.

It was mid-afternoon and there were nearly ninety miles to go to the border. Professor would gladly have given fifty dollars to be driven there, but how could he suggest such a thing to a man who was doing everything he knew to make them all comfortable, to a tall, handsome, proud man who would be insulted to be offered money for his kindness?

Birdy solved the problem by leading his father out of the room for a moment. Father and son returned arm-in-arm, and walked straight to the sunny alcove where Professor and Karin were sitting.

"Birdy and I have a visit to make near the border. We wondered if we could give you a lift. We'll use the featherbed to make a warm spot for Karin. There'll be room for Birdy and the donkey back there, too. You and I will ride in front in the cab—out of the smoke, eh, Professor? It's my brother who farms over there. I've been meaning to go see him for weeks."

How easy Birdy's father made it to say, "Thank you!" Professor and Karin moved to a round table with Birdy and his family to eat cold meat and bread and butter, pickles and cheese, cakes and biscuits. Karin watched Birdy's family, his little brother who couldn't keep still even to eat, his wispy-haired, pretty mother, his merry father— It was the first time she had seen a whole family together since she herself had been happy with her own. The joking and laughing, the mother's strokes and squeezes, the father's claps and rumplings, Birdy's teasing his little brother—all seemed to Karin another of Professor's miracles unfolding.

When its queer iron furnace was stoked, the truck belched smoke like a steam engine. Bellissimo baulked and brayed at the sight of it. Still Karin persuaded him up into the back of it. He coughed and stamped and complained as he resigned himself to traveling with his hindquarters toward the smoke. Karin and Birdy leaned against the bunker full of wood and everything that would burn. It was warm and comfortable enough, and once they started moving, the smoke would blow over their heads.

Karin had begun to look pale and ill. She dreaded reaching the Children's Village and hated the journey to be coming to an end; yet she couldn't bear to wait much longer. She had to know what would happen to Bellissimo. She didn't mind the smoke, if only it would help them to hurry. She had told Birdy's mother her fears, and the last shout she heard as they drove off was:

"And if you've any trouble over the donkey, send him back to us! We'll take care of him as long as you wish!"

Karin, waving to Birdy's mother and brother in the farmhouse door, thought that Bellissimo would have a good home with Birdy. Birdy would take care of him as well as anybody we've seen on the way. It's a funny thing, though. Bellissimo doesn't seem to like Birdy very much. He's never once nuzzled him. Oh, please, God, let Bellissimo stay with me! I love him! I want to be the one to take care of him! If only we could cross the border like the birds, gliding in a straight line as if it didn't even exist!

They rumbled and rattled over the miles to the border, over meadows and through forests, with the Rhine always close, with the dark Vosges Mountains to the west and the Black Forest to the east. Karin prayed ever more fervently as they caught sight of the white barrier stretching like a pointer across the road, as they drew up and turned into the parking place before the customs house, a gay cream-colored house not so very much bigger than a playhouse a father might build for his children at the end of the garden.

Karin drew from her pocket the four notes from Heinz Schefer, from Eric, from Brother Christopher and from Mother Beatrice. She waited in the truck while Professor took the notes into the little house. She looked neither to right nor left, but at Bellissimo's patient shaggy head drooping over the tailpiece. She would have called him to her, but Professor came back.

How worried he looked! He hurried to the cab to speak to Birdy's father.

"It looks as if we may have to spend some time here. You mustn't wait. There's a bench at the side of the house. We can wait there. The guards will help us get the donkey down. They're taking our papers to the Swiss police a little way down the road. I don't know how long it will be."

Two officials strode up. Their eyes ran over the truck, over Karin and Bellissimo. One of them held out Karin's passport and thumbed through it to compare her face with her photograph. There was no flicker of a smile on their faces.

And then she found herself sitting at Professor's side on a bench, with Bellissimo standing before her. His saddlebags were buckled on again and he couldn't come very near without bumping Karin. She had to reach far out to fondle him. They heard the rattling and rumbling of the truck turning and driving away. Birdy and his father were going to visit for an hour or so. They had promised to come back to see if everything was all right.

There was so much to talk about, so much Karin couldn't bring herself to say. She was frightened for Bellissimo most of all, but frightened, too, of the Children's Village, of the new start she must make in everything after Professor left her.

As if reading her fears, Professor said, "I haven't told you enough yet about the Village, Karin."

"Yes— Yes— I—I'm sure it's a fine place but I don't want—" The words burst from her mouth without her willing them to.

Professor took her hand.

"Why won't you take Bellissimo and me home to America with you?" she blurted out and then hung her head, wretched with shame.

"I've thought of it, Karin. I've wondered if that would be best for you," said Professor. "But I know you wouldn't be happy, not for long. I'm an old man. I'm near the end of my life. You've all your life ahead. What would happen to you when I die?"

"I wouldn't care about that," she said miserably. She gazed at him, her face very pale, her eyes blacker than he had seen them before. They sank into unhappy silence.

Finally Karin said weakly, "I'm sorry. I shouldn't have said those things."

"You should. I'm glad you did. Just try to remember I'm concerned to make the best possible life for you. I know of nowhere else in the world that could give you as much as the Children's Village. One day perhaps you'll see. . . ."

Karin managed a half-smile.

"If I can find the ball of wool we picked up on the road the other day, I could mend that hole in your sock," she said.

But there was no time for Professor to take off his shoe

and sock. A guard came around the corner and led him away. A moment later Karin saw him being driven down the road in a Volkswagen. The high-pitched whirr of its engine came back to her and then all was still. There was no one in the whole huge outdoors but Karin and Bellissimo.

She sat on the bench and patted Bellissimo. She traced his black shoulder stripe with one finger; but still dread and loneliness pressed round her like a blanket. She wished the bench were on the other side of the customs house, so she could watch for the Volkswagen's return. She gazed out over Germany. There was no sign of the truck now. Darkness was falling. A light went on inside the customs house. She hoped to see lights twinkle in nearby farms, but none came. She watched the moon rise, white and anxious-looking. Soon it hid itself behind a curtain of cloud.

Stiff and sore from her fall, from a long day of riding, Karin arched her back and crossed her good ankle over her hurt one. She shivered a little.

He didn't say how long he would be, she thought. They must have taken him to the Swiss customs house to see if the Swiss police will allow Bellissimo into Switzerland. One of the guards had a black book. That must be the book of regulations. They must be going to compare the German book with the Swiss book. Maybe the regulations say, "No animal may cross the border without exit and entry permits." That man in Aachen said it would be impossible. What shall we do if Bellissimo can't go any farther than this? I couldn't just set off and leave him, I couldn't!

Birdy's father would take him back to the farm and

maybe later on we could come back for him. But how terrible to see him being taken away! How could I make him understand it wouldn't be forever? He'd only know the hours and days were passing and I didn't come. He'd refuse to eat. He'd just bray all the time. He'd grow thinner and thinner! It would break his heart, I know it would! He'd die before we could get back to him!

To drive her dread away, she began to talk to Bellissimo.

"Nibble some grass, Bellissimo. There're some thistles over there. You used to like thistles." She tried to make her voice cheerful. "I wonder how long Professor will be. I wonder what they're saying about you. Go on now. There's a fine big thistle. I'm sure you still like them."

Bellissimo did not move. He stood meekly waiting, as close to Karin as he could get.

"If they ask me about you," she said, "if they want to know whether you're good enough to go to Switzerland, I shall tell them, 'He's a most unusual donkey! He's very clever and he loves to work and he's fond of children—'"

To herself she added, "I'd do anything for you, Bellissimo. I'd do anything to make them let me keep you!"

How awfully still it was! Nothing to hear, nothing to see but the light patches on Bellissimo, his white muzzle, the light ring around his eye, the light fur of his limbs—

"I'll count the minutes," Karin decided aloud. "No, I'll count the seconds." She counted to sixty hundreds of times. She drummed with her fingers on Bellissimo's neck, and grew more and more restless, more and more frightened.

The words so familiar in Germany since the war marched through her head. All is gone. All is lost—

She shrugged her shoulders. Other words she had not thought of before came to her, "—without a home, without a family, without Bellissimo, without anything . . ." Her chin trembled. She stroked the fur of Bellissimo's neck as if she would never stop.

"I'm an orphan. I'm nothing but an orphan. Professor's been kind to me but it doesn't make any difference. I'll be an orphan forever! They'll take Bellissimo away and then Professor will leave me and I'll be all alone in the whole world!"

Little sounds began to break into the stillness. At first they could not pierce Karin's misery. But Bellissimo heard. He stiffened. His ears pricked forward. He curved himself, twisting his neck so his head was nearer Karin. Something was creeping closer, very slowly, taking care. There was the pressing of feet on grass, the brushing of a sleeve against a wall, the sucking in of breath.

Bellissimo snorted.

Karin jumped up from the bench, half falling against the donkey's side. "What is it?" she whispered sharply. She stood taut, straining her eyes into the dark.

Above her head was a small window. It was like a giant eye staring down, focusing its beam onto the ground near the bench.

Across the beam, creeping straight toward Karin and Bellissimo, came Herr Hellmann and Herr Selbig.

Chapter 16

THEY BENT almost double as they crept past the window. They came so close that Karin could smell the cigarette smoke and feel the warmth of their breath against her face. They grinned at her and their faces were like masks. They whispered to her. That would have made it seem a game. But their questions startled her and set her heart pounding.

It was odd that soon after they stole up to her, music began to play inside the little house. There was no longer any need for Herr Hellmann and Herr Selbig to whisper so softly. Deeply distrustful, Karin hunched forward, squeezing Bellissimo's mane between her palms.

"Where's the old man?"

"Have you been through customs?"

"Have you got the donkey through?"

The questions flew at her like bullets.

"No, she stammered. "I mean—yes, I—"

"Well, where's the old man gone? He wasn't in the house when we came through. Have they taken him on to the Swiss customs?"

"Yes."

"Is there trouble with the donkey? Can't you get the donkey through?"

"I don't know."

"How long did he say he'd be gone?"

"He didn't say." Karin's good foot went up on tiptoe, her hands tightened round Bellissimo's mane. Alert but quiet, he waited to see what she wanted of him. She saw the whites of his eyes as he peered round at her. His ears lay back. His tail tuft banged against the bench in a single hard whack.

If she could climb onto the bench and jump on Bellissimo's back— But Bellissimo stood too close to her; she was wedged between the saddlebag and the bench. And there was her bad ankle. . . .

And then it was too late to run away. She felt herself being guided firmly toward the pool of light from the window.

"We've brought you a present, little girl. I have it in my suitcase. Come into the light. Kneel down and we'll open it together."

It was Herr Hellmann who led her along the cinder path before the bench to the edge of the waste patch of grass and thistles. He held his mouth close to her ear; his voice wheedled. But the grip on her arm was like a metal clamp.

He went down on one knee, pulling her with him to a kneeling position. He opened his case with his left hand, holding her fast with his right. Karin did not look into the case. She could think of nothing but Bellissimo.

She heard the crunching of the donkey's hoofs on the cinders and tried to wrench her arm free.

"What are you doing?" she cried at Herr Selbig. Her eyes

hurt from straining to look over her shoulder. She saw Bellissimo edge nimbly away.

"Be quiet, can't you?" Herr Hellmann clutched her arm tighter. "It's a fine present. I'll find it in a minute. You're a nice kid and that's why we wanted to give it to you." The wheedling came back into his voice. He ferreted among the clothing in the case.

Bellissimo shied again.

"Steady there, steady! Steady now!" came Herr Selbig's voice, low and threatening.

"Bellissimo!" Karin whimpered.

Herr Selbig's whisper was as shrill as the whistle of a singing kettle. "Can't find it! Felt down that bag a dozen times! If that old man touched it—"

"Empty the bag then!" ordered Herr Hellmann.

There were poppings of flying cinders. There was the rapping of Herr Selbig's fist against Bellissimo's neck.

"The fool animal won't stand still! Throw me your knife!"

A clasp knife flashed through the shaft of light from the window. Terror crashed inside Karin. She jerked loose and lashed out at Herr Hellmann with both arms, she butted him with her head, she kicked and writhed, defying the jabs of pain from her sprained ankle. She felt herself being backed roughly across the path to the wall of the house. Gasping and choking, she kicked out with her good leg. Her back and arms scraped the house wall. She opened her mouth to scream but Herr Hellmann's hand pushed against her face, banging her head against the wall. He hurt her face, her shoulders, her neck. She could scarcely breathe.

"Hurry up! Get that bag off, can't you?" hissed Herr Hellmann. "We'll have to make a run for it now!"

But Bellissimo went wild! Kicking and thrashing, plunging and rearing, he tore himself away from Herr Selbig. He ducked his head low and attacked with his hind legs in huge flying thrusts, sending a hail of grass and weeds far out into the road. He caught Herr Selbig with both hind legs, and sent him into a half-flip to land in a sprawling heap among the thistles.

"What the—" Herr Hellmann dropped Karin as he would a stone and sprang to pick up the knife which lay in the patch of light from the window.

Karin slipped to the ground when Herr Hellmann let her go. She lay slumped against the wall. The breath had been squeezed from her lungs and her shouts were only squeeks lost in her gasping. She saw the knife flash. In another moment Herr Hellmann would raise his arm and drive it into Bellissimo.

She raised her head and screamed. Nothing but a hoarse croak came, losing itself in the symphony, which was terribly loud now, as if the players were in a close ring around her.

Herr Hellmann crouched and jumped, clutching at Bellissimo's straps. At once Bellissimo wheeled with a jerk that sent Herr Hellmann reeling. The donkey would have galloped away had it not been for Karin. Something was wrong with her, something was hurting her. He had to stay near. He sidled nervously closer, staring at her in alarm.

Herr Hellmann scrambled to his feet and grabbed Bellissimo's straps again. Karin heard him swear in words like hot steam, "I'll kill the mangey donkey! I'll cut it to pieces!"

The knife—where was the knife? Karin's eyes strained for the slip of silver which had flashed in the light from the window. She could see Herr Hellmann's free hand now and it was wide open, there was no knife in it! He had lost the knife when he fell!

Again and again Karin tried to scream. She could rise no further than her knees because of her shaking and the pain in her neck and chest. The music from inside the house seemed softer now. Why didn't they hear, whoever they were inside?

Bellissimo lunged, slashing upward with his head. His teeth tore a rent in Herr Hellmann's jacket. He pranced, bucked and kicked, round and round in a frenzied dance, he twisted himself into narrow circles, flailing with his head and neck and tail in his fight to free himself from Herr Hellmann's grip.

But it was a cruel, unfair fight! Herr Hellmann jabbed at Bellissimo with hammer blows of his big hard fist. Blows hailed the donkey's neck, his head, his side. Often Bellissimo skidded under the blows and barely managed to right himself. What could one small donkey do against a man viciously determined to hurt him, to kill him? Bellissimo wheezed and snorted through distended nostrils, he frothed at the mouth, his eyes rolled, he tried to toss the pain from his head, from his side.

Beyond Bellissimo, Herr Selbig heaved himself to his feet, a rock grasped in one hand. Karin raised herself against the wall, her eyes glassy with fear. Her arms flew up, but fear paralyzed her legs. She opened her mouth. This time a louder cry came. Herr Selbig had hurt his foot when he fell. He limped forward, arm raised, closing in on Bellissimo.

"Karin—what is it? I heard—what?" Professor came running around the corner of the house.

Herr Selbig twisted, bracing himself on his good ankle. Professor kept coming toward Karin. He was thinking only of her.

Herr Selbig limped to one side, behind Professor. He came up behind him. Karin saw his arm lift again, high, high over Professor—

She screamed a wild warning. She lurched forward, all her pain forgotten.

Professor whirled and ducked. The rock aimed at his head knocked his hat to the ground.

Raising her head to the sky Karin screamed again. She screamed on and on, not from fear now but boldly and recklessly.

And as if sharing her new courage, Bellissimo dashed back toward her, dragging Herr Hellmann at his side. He veered sharply at the house corner, the inch required to dash Herr Hellmann against the wall. Trapped, bumped and scraped, the man landed on his shoulder and rolled over.

Two guards rushed around the corner. The light from their flashlights crisscrossed the darkness. They fell over Herr Hellmann in their anxiety to reach Professor, Herr Selbig and Karin, who were on the ground struggling, Karin on top beating with her fists on Herr Selbig because he had knocked Professor down.

"No more of that now! Back away, get back there, stand up there!"

The guards pulled haphazardly at arms and legs.

"An old man and a little girl and this one, fighting as if their lives depended on it! And that one over there— He's had a bump on the head by the look of it." The guards shone their torches and held onto their holsters. They stared from one to the other, amazed and bewildered.

To add to their confusion, everybody was shouting at once.

"The donkey's gone mad! Grab the donkey!" shouted Herr Selbig.

"Shoot it! It'll murder us all!" bellowed Herr Hellmann.

"They were trying to hurt him!" wailed Karin.

"It attacked us! We weren't doing a thing and it went for us!" cried Herr Selbig.

"These two men have attacked both the donkey and the child!" shouted Professor.

"Shoot it! Shoot it!" screeched Herr Selbig. "It'll have to be shot! Can't you see it's gone mad?"

Bellissimo thrust his dripping quivering muzzle under Karin's arm, as if to say, "The hooligans! The rascals! If they've hurt you I'll stamp them both into the ground!"

The guards stood by, still holding their holsters, as the argument rose, swift currents of words crashing into a mountainous peak.

"They were trying to get the saddlebags off Bellissimo!" cried Karin. She held onto Bellissimo and pulled herself to her feet. Every part of her ached and stung. She stood on one leg, with the toes of her sore foot brushing the ground. She held tight to her donkey's mane. She saw that Herr Selbig, too, was having trouble standing; but that did not hinder his shouting.

"That donkey's dangerous! It attacked us! We stopped to pet it and it attacked us!"

"They were trying to cut the saddlebags off! That man"— Karin pointed to Herr Hellmann—"he had a knife! He tried to hurt Bellissimo with it! It's there, over there in the grass!"

Karin won the argument. One of the guards closed in on Herr Hellmann first and emptied his pockets. The other guard searched Herr Selbig. They found no weapons, but looking through the grass with their flashlights, they found the knife.

"And now we'll tip up those saddlebags there's been so much shouting about," said one of the guards. "Watch that one, Heinrich"—he pointed with his elbow to Herr Hellmann. "This one won't go far." Herr Selbig had sat down again to nurse his sprained foot. Karin saw his mouth twitch as he muttered to himself.

Karin helped the guard to unbuckle the saddlebag straps. Bellissimo turned his head to lick her wrists. His trembling was growing less, and the sweat was drying on his body.

"Terribly wild donkey you have here, Miss," said the guard. "Wild as an African lion! And dangerous! You've only to look at it and it eats you up!"

Karin's arms smarted where they had scraped the wall. She had a goose egg at the back of her head, and grit in her hair. Her cheeks were streaked with dirt and red and aching where Herr Hellmann had pressed his fingers into them. It was a grimy smile she gave the guard.

One bag, then the other, were dumped upside down in the light from the window. Professor's belongings, the shirts beautifully laundered at St. Raphael's Hospital, lay in a muddled heap among packets of cheese and butter and bread.

A beam of light trained itself on a small leather bag tucked among the clothing from the bottom of one of the saddle-bags. Herr Hellmann shouted: "Look over there!" and rushed forward.

It was too old a trick. The guards snatched the leather bag from Herr Hellmann's hands before he could lift it from the ground.

There followed whistles of amazement. One of the guards held up a necklace which lit up the night with its radiance.

"Look here! Chock-full of jewels!"

A light was aimed into Professor's face. One of the guards demanded, "Tell us how these jewels got into the donkey's saddlebag. You've seen these men before?"

Professor described the picnic in the wood. Karin told about finding Herr Selbig bending over the saddlebag. It was easy to remember every detail; but she had no chance to finish her story. There was a scramble of boots.

"Look out! He's getting away!" It was Herr Selbig who cried the warning.

Herr Hellmann made a springing leap over the piles of clothing and scuttled around the corner of the house. The

guards pounded after him, one of them pausing long enough
to stuff the jewel bag into his pocket. The pelting of running
feet moved toward a pine grove a few hundred yards inside
Germany.

"There was a call, "Halt! Halt or we shoot!"

Karin and Professor, side by side staring into the darkness, caught their breath. A shot rang out, another. There
was no cry and now there were no footfalls. Had the guards
hit Herr Hellmann or had he got away? Or were the three
still running, far away in the wood?

Now a scuffling sounded from the road. Karin and Professor turned to see Herr Selbig limping around the front
corner of the customs house. He was running away, too, and
they were too exhausted, too overcome with all that had
happened even to call out to him to stop. They listened to
the scrabble of his feet, to the bumps and scrapings as he let
himself under the barrier. They waited for another cry of
"Halt!" for more shots.

There was no sound now except for the lovely music from
inside the house. Karin and Professor and Bellissimo were
alone at the barrier. Karin knelt down and began to refold
the tangled shirts and handkerchiefs. Professor bent forward
at her side. They folded slowly and painstakingly, and rose
stiffly every little while to take the piles to the bench, till
only the saddlebags and straps were left.

Karin reached for a strap and caught sight of her crepe-
paper crown. The moon had slid out from behind the clouds
to point up its bright flowers. It lay, not crushed at all, where
she had first struggled with Herr Hellmann. She picked it

up but did not put it on because her attention was suddenly caught by the sight of Professor's watch chain.

It was on a bare patch of ground, as if set there on display. It was intact, but the prism was gone. Only a slivver of glass still clung to the setting. A little distance away lay another splinter. Now she could see splinters everywhere, glinting up from the patch of ground, from the roots of the grasses. The prism had shattered into a thousand pieces! The magic was gone!

Chapter 17

KARIN GAVE the watch chain with its broken prism to Professor. He dropped it quickly into his jacket pocket.

"Karin," he said, "I—hate to have to tell you—"

She pulled back abruptly, closer to Bellissimo. She faced Professor as she would a stranger, as she would a thief threatening to steal her donkey. She held out her hands as if to prevent his getting past her.

He did not look at her as he gave her his message.

"They say there's no chance of our taking Bellissimo into Switzerland with us. It's there in so many words in the regulations. They can't go against the regulations. Perhaps in a few weeks, in a month or two—I could perhaps arrange for someone to come back for him—"

"I could—wait with him," she murmured, "at Birdy's farm." Her chin was trembling. Her voice quavered.

"I asked about that. I'm sure it would be all right with Birdy's parents, but it isn't all right with the border police. Oh, these regulations! Regulations! I thought this could not happen!"

They were going to take Bellissimo away from her. The

thought made Karin's eyes throb, her throat squeeze smaller. She turned away from Professor, away even from Bellissimo.

Professor had had such faith that it would be all right. He had said back in Aachen that nobody, not even a border policeman, would be mean enough to take a child's pet away from her. He had been so wrong!

"I was a fool to think it would work," he said. "I was so sure, surer than I've ever been of anything in my whole life! Oh, Karin, forgive me for building up your hopes and letting you be hurt like this! I've been a foolish old man!"

A silence settled between them. Professor became a little old, old man, bent and gray, a man Karin hardly knew. He was crushed with sadness, as he had been that day looking back over bombed Julich. His head had sunk to his chest.

Karin came back to him and touched his arm.

"Please, Professor, don't. It's all right, it will be all right in the end—at least we hope—"

His head moved slowly from side to side. How frail and ill he looked. And he had an ugly bruise on his cheek from the fight with Herr Selbig.

She put her hands on both his arms.

"Please, please—" Now she could think of nothing but Professor's sorrow that was like her own grieving for her family. She longed to comfort him.

She knelt to tie his shoelace which had come undone. She led him gently to sit down on the bench and wait for the guards' return.

There was not long to wait. Like horrid discords in the symphony still playing inside the customs house came shouts, and the thud of feet, and rough voices giving orders. Not only Herr Hellmann but Herr Selbig shuffled into the light, followed by the two guards.

"We'd no sooner caught the first one than we spotted the second. The fool thought he could get away from us across a field, lame and all, with the moon shining on him like a searchlight!"

The guards had their guns out of their holsters. They were proud and exhilarated, but also wary. Their eyes scarcely wavered from the prisoners.

"My friend here plays his Beethoven too loud," said one. "If we've told him once we've told him a hundred times to turn that radio down. He wants it like a concert hall, he says. It's a wonder we heard even a scream above that din! But he has a nose for crooks, to make up for his bad ears. Knew exactly where this one would head." The guard waved his gun at Herr Hellmann.

"It's amazing," said the second guard. "I could have sworn we'd been gone an hour, and the symphony's nowhere near finished yet. Let's get these two inside. Come on now, quick march!"

"And you, sir." The second guard addressed Professor, "Come with us. We'll show you and the little girl the biggest diamonds in Western Europe!"

Herr Selbig flashed at Karin the surly threatening look she remembered from the picnic. Bellissimo laid his ears flat and bared his teeth.

But as the procession reached the customs house door, a guard came striding along the road from the Swiss border.

Somewhere along the road he had broken off a willow branch and stripped it. He whipped it through the air as he advanced.

"I've been sent to take the donkey in charge till your friends come back with the truck, so you can get on your way," he said to Professor. He came straight to Bellissimo and stopped in surprise. He grinned at Karin.

"How do you lead the animal? There's no halter, no bridle, nothing!"

He closed his fist over Bellissimo's mane. He gave a short laugh. "Have you come all the length of Germany like this?"

Karin did not answer. Bellissimo drew back and gazed urgently round at her, showing the whites of his eyes.

"Or do you drive it by the tail?" chuckled the guard.

Again Karin gave no answer. She thought of Bellissimo's saddlebags lying at the side of the customs house. If they were strapped on, the guard would have something firmer to tug. She would not mention the saddlebags.

"Well, come on now, Nelly, giddup!" The guard tugged at Bellissimo's mane and hit him lightly on the rump with the switch.

Bellissimo refused to move. He was rolling his eyes and quivering with anxiety.

The guard gave a quick whip with the switch, still not very hard. "Giddup!" he shouted.

Somebody laughed. The guard's neck grew red. He gripped Bellissimo's mane tighter and yanked at it. The donkey only jerked his head from side to side, trying to free himself. Karin stood behind him, her fists clenched, her face white as stone. Bellissimo would have moved if she had told him to, or reached forward a little to tug at his tail tuft; but she would not do it.

The switch came down hard, once, twice, three times, on Bellissimo's rump. He had never been whipped before. Startled, he reared, snorting and whirling, throwing the guard. He began to lash out with his hind legs.

It was like the fighting beginning all over again.

The guard sat up in the road, shaking his head. Karin could see he was angry now. He got to his feet, picked up his switch and came with long slow strides toward Bellissimo.

The blare of a horn made everyone jump. The guard leaped out of the road as a shiny black car drew up to the barrier with a screech of brakes. The driver jumped out and ran around to open the car door. He saluted the elderly man who walked past Bellissimo and into the customs house. The guards followed, speaking in hushed voices, pushing Herr Hellmann and Herr Selbig indoors before them.

Again Karin, Professor and Bellissimo were alone. Bellissimo was pressing his head against Karin, nickering in his throat. She was fondling him and whispering his name, and for a moment at least, no one was taking him away.

Together the three stood, Professor wretchedly gazing down the road for sight of Birdy and his father, Bellissimo restless, his ears and body taut, Karin trembling, waiting for loneliness to begin.

I should have told Birdy all sorts of things about Bellissimo, she thought: What he likes best to eat, and about putting loads on him so he bears the weight on his back legs, and to be careful if he puts a bit in his mouth because he's not used to it now.

She whispered Bellissimo's name into his ear. Her eyes were hard and dry and too big for their sockets, and again the hurting lump in her throat refused to be swallowed.

"Don't forget," she whispered. "Somebody will come for you. Do what Birdy says. Don't forget—" But even as she said it she was sure Bellissimo would be dragged away and she would never see him again. The prism was broken. Professor's magic was gone. Nothing good could happen now, no, never again.

The guard with the switch appeared, but it was only to order Professor and Karin to come into the customs house. They moved to a spot just inside, and left the door open a crack so Bellissimo would know they were near.

Outside in the dark Professor had not noticed Karin's wild hair, her torn skirt, the gray streaks and red marks on her cheeks. In the bright light from the bulb hanging from the ceiling, he bent over her, frowning. The jewels had been poured onto the customs house desk in a breathtaking display. Professor hardly glanced at them. Instead he studied the bruises on Karin's arms and legs.

"Your arms are grazed, Karin," he murmured. "And there's a cut on your leg. Is your ankle painful? The first thing we'll do when we reach Zurich is to show that foot to a doctor." Professor was so concerned at Karin's hurts

that it didn't occur to him to be angry at Herr Hellmann
and Herr Selbig, who stood in a corner, handcuffed and
glum, their eyes red-rimmed, their faces pasty white. He did
not even notice that the conversation had stopped when he
and Karin entered the room, that everyone was staring.

Karin blinked at the jewels and looked away. The glare
and warmth of the room made her scratches and cuts smart.
Her ankle throbbed painfully. But all her pains were swallowed up in the one huge ache that sprang from her heart
and darted through her to her fingertips and toes. She
waited, shivering a little, longing to be outside with Bellissimo. How odd it was that the beautiful music still went
on playing. It seemed a lifetime since it began. The thieves
had been caught, Bellissimo and she were to be separated,
and still the music sounded, mounting up and up like a
steeple.

And how odd it was that now she was hearing the music
not only from inside the house, but from outside. It seemed
to come from everywhere, down from the sky, up from under
the earth—

The stranger stood in the center of the room. His eyes
gleamed behind gold-rimmed spectacles. He smiled across at
Karin and Professor.

"It seems there's been a great deal more than Beethoven
played here in the last hour," he said quietly. He turned
to the guards. "Ready now."

One of the guards stepped forward with a salute. He
began to describe how Herr Hellmann and Herr Selbig
had been caught.

"The little girl and the donkey were waiting outside the house, sir, and we were in here going through the regulations. It was the girl's screams that brought us running out, sir. She and the old man and one of the thieves were rolling on the ground. The other one lay in a heap. Well, sir, when we got out there we didn't know what to do, where to turn. Couldn't do much but separate them and let them talk. The truth came out all right. You'd only to listen to the girl. She knew the right of it!"

The guard took out his handkerchief and mopped his forehead. But the beads of sweat came back again as he described the escape and the recapture. He talked more and more quickly. You would have thought his whole future hung on his remembering each detail in perfect order.

The story came to an end. All around the room faces were turned toward the stranger, watching for signs of approval or blame, tense with suspense as the stranger walked round to the back of the desk and rustled through the papers lying there—the letters Karin had brought with her, her passport, Professor's passport, the books of regulations. The stranger's verdict, when finally it came, was like a great resonant bell ringing.

"The long and short of it is that this child here by the door caught these two crooks," he said. "Two of the biggest smugglers of the decade, two the police of every country of Europe have been looking for." The stranger banged his fist on the desk. The circle of faces turned to stare at Karin.

"Why take the child's donkey away from her?"

"The regulations, sir— We've studied—"

How the voice boomed! "Give me a sheet of paper!"

The stranger scribbled a message and signed his name with a flourish. He picked up every stamp on the table, pressing one after another across the top and the bottom of the paper till he had made deep borders in purple and blue and red.

He crossed the room and placed the sheet of paper in Karin's hands.

"Off you go, child, with your donkey and your good friend here—" He nodded to Professor. "And I hope you'll be very happy in Switzerland."

Karin held the paper out before her and gazed at it in wider and wider amazement.

"This is to certify that the donkey accompanying this child is to be granted immediate entry—"

There was a lightness in her head. She could not read further. Dizzy with joy, stumbling over the threshold, still holding the paper before her, she ran outside to Bellissimo.

Chapter 18

It was time to strap on the saddlebags once more. Karin and Professor packed, stopping again and again to laugh in their joy. They heard a door open and bang shut, a motor rev. They saw the black car glide smoothly away. They heard the symphony come to its close.

"It wasn't a magic prism after all!" Karin whispered in Bellissimo's ear. "The most wonderful thing of all happened after it lay broken!" She reached inside her pocket to touch the paper the stranger had given her.

Professor placed the crepe-paper crown on Karin's head. She curtsied to him with an ecstatic smile. She stiffened her upper arms and one of the guards cupped her elbows in his palms to lift her onto Bellissimo's back.

They almost forgot about Birdy and his father.

"When our friends come back in the truck—" began Professor.

"We shall look down the road to see if you're in sight, and if you are, we shall let them through the barrier to say good-by," said the guards.

Ears waving, tail flicking, Bellissimo moved out of the shadows of the customs house and onto the road. A trick of moonlight made not only his underparts but all of him look snowy shiny white. He walked with stately tread at Professor's side, across an empty stretch toward the immense, gay, sparkling cocoon of white and yellow lights that was the edges of Switzerland. There were no sounds now but the tap-tapping of hoofs and the scrunch of Professor's shoes on the pebbles.

"Who was that man?" Karin asked.

"I don't know," said Professor. "He must be a very important person. Yes—I can't believe it. It's all so amazing. Not half an hour ago we were so—so hopeless, and now—Karin, he's ordering a horse box to be sent to us!"

"To take us all the rest of the way?"

"All the rest of the way."

Karin gazed up at the sky, puzzling. She had caught Professor's habit of looking upward, as if answers to her questions would spread across the sky in cloud writing.

"He must be some sort of captain or general or something," she said. "But he wasn't wearing a uniform."

"No. It's odd. I couldn't tell who or what he was, I couldn't even be sure of his nationality."

They drank coffee and ate biscuits in the Swiss Customs House. The smoky truck, with Birdy whistling in the front, and a sleek horse box arrived from opposite directions at almost the same instant. Bellissimo, when he was installed in the horse box, hee-hawed happily. He had never before met such luxury, unless perhaps at Frau Maggold's farm. The sides of his compartment were padded to avoid bumps; there was fresh straw on the floor. His only complaint was that he could not get his head through the window to the cab. But he would be able to see Karin and wuffle at her as he munched the barley and oats provided.

In the cab of the horse box a single long leather seat gave ample space for three. Karin climbed to her place between Professor and the soldier driver. She waved to Birdy, and laughed because he kept whistling after her even when a great belch of truck smoke hid him from sight.

Five Swiss guards saw them off with a salute as big as any the German guards had given the official. The twinkling lights of Switzerland seemed to be saluting, too, and the gay houses shining in the moonlight, and the smooth ribbon highway along which they moved.

Right away Professor asked the driver about the official.

"You know as much as I do," came the answer. "All I know is he drove into our camp half an hour ago and began giving orders. I was tucked in here and off before I knew what was happening. He's a mystery to me and no mistake. V. I. P. Could make or break you with a flick of his wrist, I know that much!"

Even with her head full of questions Karin leaned back against the seat in a weariness which brought prickles to her cheeks. Her head sank to Professor's shoulder and sleep closed over her in one big lapping wave. She slept so deeply that it was almost impossible, when they reached Zurich, to rouse her enough to lead her into the apartment where she was to spend the night. Arm-in-arm with Professor and a young man in uniform, she entered a white house and climbed slowly upstairs. She smiled dreamily at the woman who washed her and helped her to undress and climb into bed.

And it was little different the next morning. She was enough awake at breakfast to realize she was in a dining room with Professor and two others; enough awake to know she was traveling in the back seat of a car; enough awake to place her foot in three positions as she was told, and to thank the doctor and nurse for cleaning her cuts and bruises and bandaging her sore ankle. She looked in fact cheerful and happy; but she was sleepwalking. It was all a dream and when she had climbed back into the cab of the horse box, and had given a long look over her shoulder to make sure Bellissimo was safe, the wave of sleep closed over her once again. She knew nothing more until Professor shook her shoulder.

"Out we get, Sleepy Head! It's time for lunch. We've reached St. Gallen. An hour for eating, another hour climbing up and up the mountains, and we'll be there!"

She let herself down from the cab. She yawned and stretched as if she would never stop. She rubbed her eyes, took one big sweeping look around—and she was wide awake, on tiptoe with eagerness. What a beautiful city St. Gallen was! White and cream, soft pink and green houses rose up the hillsides. Sunlight danced on thousands of red roofs as if the city smiled "Hello!"

Karin came awake so full of relief and joy that it would have been impossible just then for her to believe there could be sorrow anywhere in the world. She, Professor and the driver ate lunch outdoors, seated on red chairs under a striped awning. The macaroni served with the peas and veal cutlets was shaped like butterflies, the creamy cakes clustered like flowers on their three-storied dish, the ice cream turned the meal into a party.

Professor leaned back in his chair and took out his watch.

"Half-past one. Time I phoned the Village to tell them we'll soon be there."

He left his watch propped against a drinking glass. It was not his usual watch, Karin noticed. No, this was the mysterious gold watch she was sure he had found in the barn. She had not seen him bring it out before. His own must have been smashed in his fight with Herr Selbig.

Her eyes stole back to the gold watch again and again. Why, day after day through the long journey, had he said nothing about finding it? Other people found watches. They did not stuff them quickly away and say nothing, not kind, honest people like Professor.

If she were to pick up the drinking glass, the watch might flip over. That would surely not be cheating. She was thirsty. There stood a glass and near it a jug of water. It wouldn't be dishonest—would it? Her hand fluttered at the edge of the table and fell back into her lap.

"Drink of water, Karin?"

She watched the driver's hands reach out to grasp the glass and the jug. The watch rolled, spun and fell flat, directly before her eyes.

She swallowed and lowered her gaze.

The inscription read: *To Philip, on his Twenty-first Birthday, with Love from Dad.*

"Do you want a drink of water or don't you?" The driver was smiling at her genially, holding the glass and the jug poised.

"Oh—yes, please."

Could the soldier in the barn have been Professor's son? Her friend, the young man she had laughed with and liked so much and tried so hard to help, the one who had promised to come back to find her, was named Philip. But if so, why had Professor never told her?

Her thoughts whirled, tumbling over themselves.

Why was she suddenly so sure Philip was Professor's son? What had happened to make her sure? Nothing had changed. Professor had picked up a watch in a barn and put it in his pocket. Anyone might have done that. And Professor had never mentioned a son. Maybe he had no son at all.

But she trembled in the excitement of her discovery, she was sure, she was utterly and positively sure!

She must face Professor at once, before they reached the Village and Professor went away and it was too late! She must ask him why he had never told her, not even when they stood in the barn, in almost the exact spot where the soldier had lain, the day they began their journey.

Gingerly Karin pushed the watch back a few inches, so Professor would not be startled when he returned. Tingling with eagerness, she watched the old man take his place opposite her. Frightened, she heard the driver excuse himself, saying he would meet them at the horse box in five minutes. Terrified, she stared into Professor's face.

"Professor—"

"Yes, Karin?"

"I—just wondered—" Her voice failed. Oh, it was worse, much worse than asking if Marianne could come to the Children's Village! "Please—why didn't you tell me it was your son—Philip—in the barn?"

There was a quick gasp, a long drawn-out breath, and silence. Now she couldn't look at Professor. For an age she was afraid to go on.

"I don't know how it is I guessed," she whispered. "It just came to me when I read the inscription on the watch. Why didn't you want me to know? I told you all about him. Why didn't you tell me he was your son?"

She had to wait a long time for the answer.

"I didn't tell you, Karin, because I didn't want to add to your—your sense of loss."

How hard it was for Professor to speak. Why?

Karin glanced up and knew why.

"Because he's dead."

Professor nodded.

"Now you know, and I may as well tell you the rest. He came back and lay there—at home with me—helpless, blind—"

"Blind?"

"You didn't know he was blind. Even in the barn—"

"No!" Karin's fingers flew up to her mouth.

"Right up until he died he was—well, I can never think of my son without wanting to be twice the man I am!"

A huge shiver rocked Karin from head to foot.

"Please—I shouldn't have—I'm so sorry—"

She wanted to jump up and run to Professor, to put her arm round his shoulders and her cheek against his to comfort him; but people at nearby tables were staring now, whispering about them.

"Philip wouldn't have wanted you to know all this. I'm sorry I've had to tell you." Professor sat very still, his head bowed.

"Thank you," breathed Karin. "I—did he—did he ask you to come and find me?"

Professor gave her a long look.

"He had no need to ask, Karin."

She wanted to cry, to sob out loud. She gave the smallest whispered exclamation and hung her head. Silently they left the restaurant and climbed back into the horse box to travel the last lap of the journey, up the mountains to the Children's Village.

Chapter 19

THE HIGHER the horse box climbed, the more the sunlight sparkled, the thicker the flowers grew, the more merrily the birds sang.

"Grüss Gott!" A farmer called the "God bless" from the roadside, a primrose dangling from his mouth. They were so high now that sometimes they drove through a cloud, and sometimes a cloud drifted by below them.

Karin swallowed to relieve the pressure in her ears. During the journey she had thought very little about her destination. Nothing had mattered so much as keeping Bellissimo. Since crossing the border, she'd been too sleepy to think at all.

Till now. The children she was to meet very soon and live with and grow to know—would they want to know her? She recalled what Professor had said about them. They were from many countries, and they, like her, had lost their parents in the war. She could blame the Russians for killing her father, the British for killing her mother and her sister. But some of the children in the Village must blame the German soldiers for killing their families. Maybe some

of the children wouldn't want a German to live in their Village—

Professor was nudging her.

"Look through the side window, Karin. We're very near now. It's just there, up ahead. Round the next bend we should see it—if those clouds aren't hiding it."

They swept round the mountain.

"There, past that little forest! See the roofs! There!"

Before them, still higher up, hung a white batting cloud, and rising out of it was a cluster of houses with rows of windows that were long, thin gold bars in the sun. You couldn't see the ground underneath the houses at all. It seemed a fairy village built on a layer of cloud, high in the sky.

They came to a stop because there was danger of sticking fast in the muddy track leading up the mountain. They brought Bellissimo down the comfortable ramp out of the horse box, strapped on his saddlebags and followed the track past the last houses of Trogen—and higher still to the first houses of the Children's Village.

They were handsome houses, much bigger and finer than Karin had imagined.

Professor beamed across at her.

"One day you'll go away from here and you'll come back and say, 'Oh, it's wonderful to be home!' See, Karin, see the little porches and terraces and the flower beds—and there's the Square. See the half-built house there. That's for the English children. Over there, that one not yet finished, that's to be for the Austrians. But how odd it is to see no children about! They're usually bounding up and down the hills like jack rabbits. It means they've begun the concert. They told me about it when I phoned. It's over there in the Old Farmhouse. We'll creep in quietly and watch from the back."

Professor quickened the pace, making himself shorter and shorter of breath; but still he went on talking.

"That's the Office." He pointed as they hurried across the Square. "I slept in that building, up on the second floor, when I was here a few days ago. And there—there, Karin—is your house! The one with the balcony. Look, they've made a garden already. They've been busy while I've been away. And this"—they were crossing a hussocky field—"this is the football ground until they can level a better one. And look down, Karin. You can see all the little villages from here, Speicher and Rhetobel and Trogen, of course, and Wald. Down there is Lake Constance, and there's Germany. We've come all that long way, all that long, long way!"

Quickly, and so quietly that not a soul noticed, they entered the Old Farmhouse. Professor and the soldier driver went in first. Bellissimo followed at Karin's heels, straight inside without hesitation.

There were the children! There, seated in rows in the semi-darkness, in one huge high-ceilinged room, were hundreds of children! They were silent and rapt, their faces lifted. On the stage before them danced a circle of girls. They whirled and stamped in their bright costumes. When they stopped dancing and bowed, Karin saw that their costumes were French. They were dressed almost exactly like the second figures on Bellissimo's saddle-bags.

The dancers left the stage. The audience clapped and stamped their feet. The little orchestra of boys and girls down in front struck up a different melody, a slow stately tune in a minor key. In came the Greek dancers. Karin knew at once they were Greek, like the fourth figures on the saddlebags.

After the Greeks came the Poles, then the Italians. Karin recognized them all. It was as if she were dreaming again by the little pool near Globkes' farm.

When the lights went up, the children on stage caught sight of Bellissimo. A whisper, a murmur, a buzz, then a shout went up.

"Look, a donkey!"

"It's a donkey!"

"A real live donkey!"

Everyone in the audience turned to see what the excitement was about. Children laughed and called and waved. The little ones jumped up and down.

The tall, white-haired man who was conducting the orchestra raised his hands and the whole assembly, performers and audience, began to sing at the top of their lungs. It was a merry song, full of shouts of "Bravo!" It ended with three mighty "Bravo's!" and then a bedlam of shouting broke out. There were cries of "Bring the donkey onto the stage!"

There was only one way to stop the noise. Professor

walked down the side aisle to the platform, drawing Karin with him. Bellissimo followed close behind, mounting the steps to the platform as if he climbed steps every day. In the noise of the Old Farmhouse he would have tried to climb a ladder to stay near Karin.

The white-haired man shook hands with Professor and kissed him on both cheeks. Professor turned to the audience, raised his hand and silence fell, a silence so complete that Karin could hear Bellissimo's breathing.

"It's wonderful to be back here in my favorite place in all the world, among this fine big family again," began Professor. "We have had a long hard journey, Karin and her donkey and I. It's been a journey full of adventures and dangers, and full of marvelous surprises!"

Professor put his arm around Karin's shoulders and drew her closer. A sea of eyes turned to her, studying her bandaged arms and legs, her foot in its clumsy bandage, her flower crown—

"You will be proud to have Karin in your Village. And Bellissimo! What village wouldn't count itself lucky to have a donkey like Bellissimo!"

There was a thunder of applause. The concert was over. Children tried to push forward to touch Bellissimo. A dozen grownups had hurried onto the stage to speak to Professor, and there was no room.

Professor bent down to Karin.

"Take Bellissimo through the little door behind the stage. It leads to the side of the Farmhouse. You'll find four linden trees in a row. Wait there and I'll bring your house parents to meet you. I must make arrangements about Marianne."

Professor was surrounded by smiling people. Everybody seemed to know him, to want to speak to him. Karin threaded her way, Bellissimo close behind, among the crowd and through the door.

She waited for Professor under the first of the four trees. She wondered how it was that everybody seemed to know him and like him.

"I know why," she whispered to Bellissimo. "It's because he's the finest, dearest old man in the whole world, that's why!"

She would have to get used to living without him, perhaps never to see him again!

She looked timidly out across the Village. In little groups the Village children were crossing the football field toward the Square. Two small boys zigzagging across the field caught sight of Bellissimo and came back a distance to stand and grin. Another group halted at the Farmhouse corner. A blond boy began to talk excitedly. His arms flew into the air. He paced back and forth and pointed toward the linden trees. Karin knew he was talking about her. The others with him, two boys and a girl, stared at Karin and Bellissimo as they listened.

Karin went cold with foreboding. One arm thrown across Bellissimo's withers, she limped backward, easing the donkey back past the second and third trees, and around behind the fourth tree. She hid between Bellissimo and the tree and did not look out. She could hear long striding steps drawing

nearer, nearer, and the fainter steps of the blond boy's
companions hurrying away in the opposite direction. Karin
clung tightly to Bellissimo. Her cheeks flamed. Her breathing came fast with dread.

He stole along the edges of the boles of the trees, and
halted a few feet from Karin and Bellissimo. He stood, legs
apart, dangling in his fingers the cord of a whistle. Karin
lifted her eyes in a darting glance. The boy was scowling.
One of his eyes drooped unnaturally and a dark scar ran all
the way across his forehead.

"You Germans!" he muttered fiercely. "You make trouble
wherever you go! You killed all my family, my father, my
mother and my brother! You killed my brother before my
eyes!"

"I—I?" faltered Karin. "I lost—"

"I hate you! We don't want Germans here! Go away!
Go back where you came from!"

The boy caught sight of Professor stepping through the
side door of the Old Farmhouse. He whipped around and
ran. His friends were far away now, at the other side of the
football field.

In a daze of anguish Karin leaned against Bellissimo. She
did not hear Professor approaching, bringing her house
parents to meet her. Her chin trembled, her throat ached.
This, then, was the end of all her hopes, all her longings, all
the days of walking, all the dangers and hurts. She must
get on Bellissimo and they must ride away, fast, hiding in
the crowds—

But where? Where could they go? The words that had
come to her at the border returned, louder, more viciously:

"Without a home, without a family, without anything. I'm an orphan, I'm nothing but an orphan! I will be an orphan forever! I'm all alone in the whole world!"

She buried her face in Bellissimo's soft side. She dug her fingernails into her palms. She cowered, bowed in dejection.

"Here she is, here's our Karin! Karin, I've brought your house parents to meet you! Where are you? Bless you, you're right out of sight behind Bellissimo! This is Herr and Frau Riegger."

Professor had his arm around her. She tripped and stumbled as he brought her out into the sunshine. She rubbed her face quickly with her sleeve and struggled to look up. She clenched her teeth to stop her chin from trembling. She didn't dare to look straight at the house parents. She couldn't bear it if Professor noticed anything. She couldn't bear it if he found out about that boy.

Shakily she shook hands and curtsied, first to Frau Riegger, then to Herr Riegger.

"She's shown such courage—all along the way! It would take me a week to tell you what a grand little traveler she's been. Do you know, back in Aachen there was a poor old woman, a Frau Lang—"

Karin turned her eyes away, steeling herself.

Professor noticed. Quickly he turned everyone's attention to Bellissimo.

"And this creature here," he said, "has tried all the length of Germany to have my mustache for dinner!"

Karin felt a soft little hand on her wrist and heard a tiny, deep, husky voice saying, "Gee-gee."

She went down on one knee to the sound. She looked up sideways at a chubby, rosy little girl.

"Gee-gee," said the voice again wistfully. "Nice Gee-gee."

The little girl hardly saw Karin. She stood rapt, her chin sharply raised, her fat arms outstretched, her eyes round with wonder. Her cheeks, her whole face had grown pink— exactly as Gerti's used to do when something pleased her tremendously. Karin's mother would say, "Look at that child, blushing with joy again!"

Tenderly Karin put her mouth to the little girl's ear.

"Do you want to pat the Gee-gee?" she whispered.

"Pat Gee-gee. Pat Gee-gee," chirped the little girl.

Karin picked her up and carried her to Bellissimo. It was exactly like carrying Gerti, the same weight, the same fat solid middle, the same soft arm thrown round her neck.

"Gee-gee's ear," said Karin. "Gee-gee's eyes. Gee-gee's mouth, Gee-gee's tongue—" The child repeated the words after her as she touched Bellissimo. She gave a sudden loud, throaty chuckle.

"Gerti loves the Gee-gee!" she laughed.

Gerti! The little girl's name was Gerti!

Happiness could do what sorrow could not. For the first time in many months, for the first time since before she had lost her family, Karin burst into tears.

She hid her face against Gerti's neck and sobbed. She had not cried the night at Globkes' farm when she thought she must leave Bellissimo behind. All through the long journey she had not once cried, not even when she walked over the rubble that had been her home in Julich, nor during the hours of anxiety and fear at the border. But now she cried and could not stop. Tears rolled down her cheeks and she kept wiping and wiping them away. All the while she lifted Gerti onto Bellissimo's back, all the while Professor and the house parents and she guided Bellissimo away from the linden trees and across the football field, she wept.

The dancers and singers, pouring last of all out of the Old Farmhouse and across the field, saw Bellissimo carrying Gerti on his back. They crowded around, they draped Bellissimo with the flower chains they had used in their dancing. In their bright costumes they formed a procession, laughing and singing their way across the Village toward the German House.

It was a triumphal procession. As they drew up before the balcony, Karin was singing with them a song she knew well—"All the Children are Here." The tears were drying on her cheeks and she was raising her chin and singing as loudly as anyone. One boy had said he hated her and didn't want her in the Village. Dozens and dozens of boys and girls were smiling at her and welcoming her!

Bellissimo felt welcome, too. He rolled up his lip, tossed his head and gave a deep, raspy, hoarse laugh.

"He's laughing! The donkey's laughing! Look at him, laughing his head off!" cried the children. "Oh, Bravo! Bravo, Bellissimo!"

But in the midst of Karin's new joy Professor left her. He made a final little speech to the house parents.

"I must tell you there have been times on the journey when I've thought I was surely traveling with one of God's angels!

I've always thought it was important to die first in order to be an angel, but I found myself wondering—"

Karin could not take her eyes from Professor's face.

"I—thought the same about you!" she whispered.

She and Professor stroked Bellissimo, one at each side of him, leaning against him, wanting to be the old trio as long as they could. Karin tried to smile.

"I—I'm glad your mustache is still whole," she managed to say. "I'm glad about—everything!"

There was a flash. Karin's heart skipped a beat. The prism— But no, Professor had brought out the gold watch and the sun had caught it as he held it in his palm. He slipped it into her hand and closed her fingers over it.

"He'd want you to have it," he said.

Holding Karin by the hand, Professor started to walk away from the German House.

"Take good care of Bellissimo," he said. "I want to find him healthy and fat when I come to visit you next summer!"

Karin threw both her arms around Professor's neck and kissed him. The tears started again as she watched him touch his hat to everyone gathered before the German House and walk away with the soldier driver, downhill to the horse box.

"Good-by, Professor! Good-by," she whispered softly, gazing after him through eyes stinging with tears. Her heart felt to be swelling, swelling, to be going to burst with joy and sorrow mixed. She squared her shoulders, rubbed her eyes once more, took a deep breath and limped back to Bellissimo. With her arm again around Gerti on Bellissimo's back, she pressed her forehead against her donkey's furry neck. Her whisper was lost in the noise of the crowd, but Bellissimo heard:

"This is home, Bellissimo, we've come home!"